ABOUT THE AUTHOR

Lexie Winston has been an astronaut, rock star, princess and time traveller. In her dreams. But none of the dreams have lived up to what becoming an author has been like. She gets to live in a world of pure imagination, and her heroines get to do the things she's always wished she could.

When not writing books, Lexie is a mother of two gorgeous teenagers and the wife to a patient and understanding man. They live in Western Australia and are lorded over by a black toy poodle. She loves camping, reading and if her iPad was stolen, her world would explode. (It has the kindle app on it.)

And check out my website at lexiewinston.com

And you can find all my links at
https://linktr.ee/LexieWinston

ALSO BY LEXIE WINSTON

The Collectors Division

(Paranormal Reverse Harem Series)

Guardian

Guardian's Blood

Guardian Ascending

Collector's Division Omnibus

Neighpalm Industries Collective

(Enemies to Lovers Reverse Harem)

Abandoned Girl

Broken Girl

Tormented Girl

Wanted Girl

Cherished Girl

Loved Girl

Superficial Girl - Jacinta's Story Part 1

Superficial Girl - Jacinta's Story Part 2

Seductive Sins Collection

(Reverse Harem Series)

Glorious Gluttony

Gangs, Guns, and Glory

Galaxy Circus

(Sci-Fi Reverse Harem Series)

Apprentice

Stagehand

Whisperer

A Night Most Wicked - Galaxy Circus Novella

A NIGHT MOST WICKED

A Galaxy Circus Novella

LEXIE WINSTON

First published by Neighpalm Publishing in 2022

A Night Most Wicked

Mobi format: 978-0-6453753-6-7
Print: 978-0-6453753-7-4

Cover design by Raven Ink Designs
Edited by Elemental Editing

❀ Created with Vellum

CHAPTER ONE

Susie

The lights of Vegas twinkle in our rearview mirror as Mark and I head out of the city. "Can you believe the special effects they used? And the animatronics were out of this fucking world," Mark comments, raving about the circus we'd just seen. I didn't think I was going to be able to drag him away.

My best friend Lila recently discovered that she's not alone in the world and has a family that runs a circus. We just spent the weekend catching up with her and seeing the show—one that included a great big animatronic dinosaur that just lumbered up Las Vegas boulevard for publicity. We left Lila behind to deal with that and headed out of the city.

I feel an indulgent smile lift my lips at my

boyfriend's enthusiasm. I think if Lila's grandpas had offered him the job of circus doctor, he would have jumped at the chance. Unfortunately for him, they already have one, and he just so happens to be one of Lila's new boyfriends. Yes, you heard right, one of. I can't tell you how surprised I was when my best friend told me she was in a poly relationship. While not necessarily vanilla, Lila had never seemed to be interested in any steady relationship, let alone one with multiple men, but I guess life throws you curveballs when you least expect it.

I had a curveball of my own thrown at me this weekend when my partner of nearly a year admitted that he was bisexual. I'm kind of sad that he didn't think he could share that with me, but I guess I've never really shared my own bisexual experiences with him. Nobody likes to hear about their partner's exes. It's probably something we need to talk about in depth, but I'm not entirely sure how to bring the subject back up. Maybe I'll just bury my head in the sand for a little longer.

I really love Mark. Although this started as a quick fuck in the on-call room to blow off some steam, it's developed into more, and I'm not sure if I'm ready to rock the boat with some difficult questions.

"Lila looked really happy, didn't she?" I sigh, and I see him look at me out of the corner of my eye before he reaches out and grabs my hand, giving it a squeeze.

"Yeah, babe, she really did. But that doesn't mean she doesn't miss you or she's going to forget you. She's on an adventure, but you will always be a part of her life even if you don't see each other every day."

And this is why I love the man. He just intuitively knows what I'm thinking.

I hear myself sigh loudly again. "I know. It's just that life has changed so much, and I guess I'm struggling to wrap my head around the fact. Lila has always floated through life with no direction, and I like being her port in the storm so to speak. Now she has other friends, and what if she doesn't need me anymore?"

He reaches out and pulls me across the bench seat of our rental, tucking me into his side. The classic Cadillac has made this ride so much more enjoyable, being able to ride next to him all the way with the wind in my hair and his arm around me. I feel a little like Sandy from *Grease*. "Aww, babe, she's always going to need you. And just because the two of you aren't living in each other's pockets anymore isn't going to change that, and none of her new friends are going to replace you. I promise." He kisses the side of my head, keeping his eyes on the road the whole time. Mark always knows exactly the right thing to say to make me feel better. He's always been a little funny around Lila, but now that it's all out in the open, we can move forward. They seemed to be getting along much better during our stay, and I can't say I wasn't relieved. I didn't want to give either of them up, but Mark was always so awkward around her. I thought that maybe he was hot for her, so it was a big relief to know that wasn't what the problem was.

My thoughts drift to imagining what my boyfriend looked like loving another man, and I squirm in my seat as those images flash into my mind. I've always had a vivid imagination, and I can't say I hate anything that I see in my mind right now.

"Are you okay? You're squirming." Mark glances down at me before looking back at the road.

"I was just thinking about your revelation from the weekend," I tell him, trying desperately to hide the lust these thoughts have inspired.

"Oh?" There's a hint of concern in his voice, and I rub my hand against his thigh reassuringly. My hand brushes against the bulge in his pants, and I feel it twitch under my palm.

"Yeah, I'm sad you didn't feel like you could tell me about it. Why is that?"

He shrugs his shoulders, not looking at me. "I don't know, babe. At first, it didn't really matter. We were only fucking at work, you know?" I nod my head in complete understanding. "And then when it became more, I couldn't quite work out how to slip it into the conversation."

"Maybe something like, 'Hey, Susie, just so you know, while 1 love your tits and pussy, I also like

4

having cock up my ass,'" I tease him, and thankfully he chuckles. "Or, I don't know, if you had suggested pegging in the bedroom, it might have given me a better idea as well."

His eyes widen in amazement, and he looks at me. "You would have been interested in that?" he asks, sounding stunned, and I frown.

"Have we really been that vanilla?" I think back over the year we've been together, and my mouth drops open in astonishment. We really have been that vanilla. We have had lots of good sex, but it was all very standard stuff—missionary, doggy, reverse cowgirl. We haven't played, and there haven't been any toys or trying new things. I guess we're both so busy that we grab what we can get when we can get it.

I turn so that my body is facing him and my knee is up on the seat between us. "Let's make each other a promise now. No more just grabbing sex when we can get it. Let's make a pact to spice up our sex life. I am open to all the experimenting you want to do, and we need to stop making do. As spectacular as the sex is, if we don't keep it fresh and interesting, I'm worried we'll get into a routine, and I'm almost a hundred percent certain that's enough to kill a relationship."

"Yeah, okay. That sounds good to me." He nods enthusiastically, and I have a naughty thought, but instead of pushing it away like I might have in the past, I decide to follow through with it. Looking behind me, I check if there are any cars behind us. I can see a dark vehicle, but it's a good distance away, so I doubt they can see what I'm doing. I reach over and open up his pants. His eyes widen in surprise as I reach in, pull out his cock, and lick the tip. It's half hard from our conversation, but it quickly becomes fully erect under my attention.

"Oh fuck," he mutters, biting his lip as I swirl my tongue around the head. I smile up at him, and he mumbles, "I'm going to kill us if you keep doing that."

"Well, you better keep your eyes on the road and your hands on the wheel then," I reply before taking him back into my mouth. He tastes slightly salty, but it doesn't bother me as I make him nice and wet so my hand slides easily up and down his length. Mark's cock is big, and it takes a bit of effort for me to get it into my throat. I have to work it with both my hand and my mouth, but I get a good rhythm going, and I feel Mark's thigh muscles quiver as he tries to hold back his release. One of his hands drops into my hair, threading through the strands and holding on tight. He helps me up and down, muttering dirty words to me.

"That's it, baby. You suck my cock so good." A truck barrels by, tooting its horn, but I don't care. It's mostly dark now, and the driver won't be able to see much. Pulling back, I lap up the salty precum leaking from his head, swirling my tongue around the underside before engulfing it again and humming. "Fuck, I'm going to come," he warns, and I lower my head farther so I can swallow his salty load straight down. He thrusts twice and groans long and loudly as he finds his release. I swallow it, but there's a lot, and I feel some of it leak out the sides of my lips. Once I know he's finished, I pull back, cleaning him up before tucking him away, his length still hard. I sit up and go to wipe my mouth, but he palms the back of my head and pulls me to him, kissing me hard as he keeps his eyes on the road. His tongue licks across my lips, catching all of the cum that leaked out, and my mouth drops open in shock as I pull away.

There's a smirk on his face, and he winks at me. "I don't mind a bit of cum," he reminds me, and a shiver of desire runs down my spine as I think about him sucking another guy's cock. Now I'd like to see that.

My hair is blowing all over the place now that it's not covered by the scarf I had in it. I feel around behind me to find where Mark had pushed it when he'd threaded his hands into my hair. Not finding it, I look down at the footwell and see it under one of Mark's shoes, so I lean in and grab it. Just as I sit up again, the car lurches, and I'm flung around.

"Fuck." I grab Mark's thigh, trying to stop myself from bashing my head on the steering wheel.

"Shit, Susie, hang on," Mark yells as he wrestles with the wheel.

I scramble to put my seat belt back on, but the

car is swerving so much I can't get stable. I'm thrown back and forth across the seat, and an explosion of pain makes me see stars as my head bounces off the dashboard in front of me. I slump into the passenger side footwell as I watch Mark smash his foot against the brake, but it doesn't seem to be working well. We're slowing, but not as fast as we should.

"Fuck, fuck. Brace yourself!" Mark shouts, and I feel the car leave the road.

I scrunch my eyes tight, waiting for the pain, but there's no big impact, just the sounds of branches scraping against the side of the car before we come to a lurching stop. When I open my eyes, I can see that Mark is okay. He has a wild, slightly unhinged look on his face as he grips the steering wheel tightly with both hands, and he's breathing heavily.

He releases the wheel and looks around, running his hands through his black hair as he breathes out a sigh of relief before his gray eyes find mine and his brow wrinkles with fear.

"Oh my god, Susie, are you okay?" He scrambles to undo his belt as I feel a trickle of something on my face. Lifting a shaky hand to it, I swipe at the offending liquid, and I'm surprised to see blood when I pull away. I stare at it, knowing I'm probably in shock. When Mark gets his belt undone, he slides across the bench seat and holds out a hand. Taking it, I let him pull me out of the footwell, grimacing at the aches and pains I'm feeling from being thrown around the car.

"What happened?" My voice is a little shaky, and my teeth start to chatter.

"I don't know. I think we might have blown a tire." Mark runs his hands over my body, looking for injuries, before taking my head between his hands and examining the cut on my temple. He pokes at it, and I hiss, drawing in a breath. He scrunches up his nose. "Sorry. I think you might need a stitch or two." He uses his shirt to wipe away the blood that's now running rapidly down my face.

Reaching over me, he opens the glove box and pulls out a pack of tissues. "Here, hold some of these over it while I look at the damage to the car. I think we need to go back to Vegas and get you looked at." He's pretty calm now that we've stopped moving, but with his emergency room training, that's not really a surprise.

I watch as he climbs over into the back seat and slides over the trunk onto the ground. We left the top down because I wanted to look at the stars on the drive back to LA, but now it makes an easy escape hatch since the front of the car seems to have come to a stop in a bush, making getting the doors open problematic.

My head is throbbing, so I lean it back on the seat as I wait for Mark to assess the damage. He doesn't need my help, and I don't really feel like moving. I close my eyes as I listen to him make his way around the car, the scrape of his shoes against the gravel loud in the silence. Now that the car is off, it's almost pitch black out here, and there isn't another car in sight. Mark is using his phone light to assess the damage, and I can hear him muttering to himself, but I don't have the energy to ask what's wrong. He'll let me know when he's ready.

I must drift off, because he gently shakes me awake. "Hey, baby, don't close your eyes. You might have a concussion." He's climbed back in and is in the seat next to me.

"How's the car?" I ask, my words slightly slurred, and Mark's frown deepens.

"Somehow, we've punctured two tires, it's why I couldn't keep control of the car, so even if I changed one, I still couldn't get us out of here. Not to mention I think a branch pierced the radiator, since there's a puddle of liquid under the hood."

"We'll just call a tow truck. We have insurance," I suggest, and he heaves out a big sigh.

"I tried, but I have no reception."

"Huh, that's weird. Let me check mine." I lean forward to grab my phone out of my purse, but grimace as a wave of pain intensifies in my head. Groaning, I grab hold of it and squeeze my eyes shut in the hope it will ease.

"Let me do it." He reaches over and grabs my bag, dragging it into his lap. He feels around until he brings out my phone. Mark holds it up, but I can tell by his groan that I don't have any either.

"Crap," he mutters, and I feel my eyes drift closed again. "No, sweetie, come on. Let's get you out of the car. I saw lights just before we ran off the road. We can walk back and see if they have a phone we can use."

Mark shakes me awake and helps me climb over the seat and then slide down off the trunk. I grimace in pain as my feet hit the ground and sway slightly. He wraps his arm around me, and I finally look around. We're in a wooded grove of some kind, and the bush we hit is a small pine tree.

"Where are we?" I ask my boyfriend as he starts moving us forward. My purse is over one of his shoulders, and he's wrapped his arm around me to help me.

"Remember that weird gothic mansion we saw on the way, and how it was surrounded by a forest? I think this is that forest. The time frame fits, we've been driving for about an hour."

"Oh, and you think the lights are the mansion? What was it called… the Pleasure Inn?" That distracts me from the pain slightly. "They should have a phone we can use."

Suddenly, thunder flashes and lightning cracks across the sky, lighting up the woods. I can see Mark briefly before it fades again. His eyes are wide with surprise, just like mine are at the unexpected sound and light.

"Crap, where did that come from? The sky was perfectly clear when we left Vegas, and I didn't notice it getting stormy, did you?" I ask him, and I can just make out him shaking his head.

"No, come on. We better hurry, otherwise we're going to get drenched." Just as he says that, the skies open up. Water starts to pour down, and even with the cover of the trees, we're soon soaked through.

We left the top down on the convertible, thank goodness we have insurance.

My teeth are chattering, and goosebumps cover my exposed flesh as we continue to stumble through the forest toward a faint glow in the distance. That has to be the mansion, or at least somewhere we can take cover and hopefully make a call.

CHAPTER TWO

Susie

I'm not sure how long it takes us to make it through the forest, but it finally opens up to a sealed driveway. In front of us are two large, wrought iron gates built into a stone wall that appears to surround the property. The gates have a P on one side and an I on the other. A blinking red light catches my eye, and when I look up, I notice a camera sitting on top of the wall. Before I can say anything to Mark about it, there's another crack of thunder and a brilliant flash of light, and I squeal in fright as a tree explodes not twenty yards away. Wood chips fly through the air, narrowly missing us as the tree falls down across the driveway, taking out power lines and blocking the exit. The wire flips around, sparking like crazy.

"Fuck, we need to get out of this storm," Mark calls out over the wind that is suddenly howling through the trees. Although the gates are closed, Mark yanks on one, but it doesn't budge. I look around for a call box or an automatic eye. There has to be something that triggers these gates.

Mark climbs up onto the gates and uses his full weight as he leans back, and suddenly, one opens just enough for us to slide through. He jumps down, holding out his hand. "Come on, baby."

His hand is warm as I place mine in it. The rain starts to hurt as the wind blows, so we keep our heads down and run toward the gothic mansion. There are lights blazing in some of the windows and a few cars parked out front as we scramble up the steps to the front door. Again, lightning lights up the sky, illuminating the building in front of us. It's so dark and scary looking, it wouldn't appear out of place on the set of a horror film. Again, another flashing light draws my eye upward, and there's a camera pointing at the step. On the front door is a big door knocker in the shape of a…

"Is that an alien door knocker?"

Mark and I both lean closer to get a better look. Sure enough, it's shaped like a stereotypical little green alien. It's made of brass or copper, so it has a green tint to it, and it has a ring in its mouth for us to use to knock.

Mark snorts in amusement. "I guess we are in

Nevada. Area 51 isn't that far away." He reaches up and bangs it against the door. It makes a loud sound, and hopefully someone is inside to hear it.

I shudder with cold, and he wraps his arms around me and presses a kiss to the side of my head, avoiding the cut. The bleeding has slowed, but I'm not sure if it's due to the rain and cold or if it's not as bad as Mark initially thought. I'm sure once we get inside and can get some proper light on it, he'll know more.

"What's taking them so long?" I ask between chattering teeth, and he huffs an annoyed sound before reaching for the knocker again, but a light turns on above us and the door opens wide.

"Welcome to the Pleasure I—" The man stops his enthusiastic greeting, and his mouth drops open in shock. He looks us up and down before peering behind us.

While he's doing this, I use his distraction to get a good look at him. He's fucking gorgeous. He's wearing a tuxedo with tails but has no shirt underneath, and we can see the swirls of silver tribal tattoos covering a well-defined chest and abs. He has long indigo hair which is shaved at the sides, exposing more tribal tattoos on his skull, and is tied back, and there's a top hat covering it. Silver rings line both ears, as well as in his eyebrow and his bottom lip. He has sharp cheekbones, with eyes that look to be purple, and pouty lips that are just asking to be bitten. He's sex on legs, and a wave of guilt flows through me as I realize I'm ogling him while my boyfriend keeps me warm, but when I look at Mark to see if he noticed, I see he's eyeing him with a look of awe as well.

"You're not the Jelliad delegation." He steps back slightly, his eyes widening before he hisses. "You're human. How did you get in here?" he demands, his eyes narrowing as he takes in our drowned figures.

Human? What was he expecting? Aliens? Maybe he's a little eccentric. I mean, there was the door knocker…

"Yeah, hi, I'm Mark, and this is Susie, and we had a car accident. We have no cell service. I was wondering if we could use a phone to call a tow truck and maybe use your first aid kit. Susie is injured." My boyfriend puts on a smile that tends to win over even the most difficult of patients, but the guy keeps staring at us.

He ignores Mark's question. "You didn't say how you got in."

I feel Mark stiffen slightly in annoyance, and I pat him on the chest, trying to stop him before he says anything to upset our host.

"The front gate opened for us. We just walked up the drive," I tell him, and his eyes narrow even more until he's squinting at us. Again, his gorgeous purple eyes run the length of each of us. I feel the urge to stick my tongue out, but then my body grows slightly warm, and I start to worry that maybe I'm getting a fever from the cold. The heat slowly dissipates, however, and the guy's eyes widen and his eyebrows jump.

"Hmm, interesting," he mutters to himself before nodding. "Of course, come right in, and I'm sure we can help you out." Gone is the suspicious look, and in its place is a blinding, dazzling smile. He steps back and waves us in like a game show host, bowing down and tipping his top hat.

Mark and I hustle in out of the rain, and the big wooden door slams shut ominously behind us. The house is warm and inviting, with sumptuous decorations and lavish furniture. Red, gold, and black hold a lot of importance in the color scheme. Somewhere within the house, it sounds like a party is going on with laughter and music. There's a reception desk inside the foyer, and the gorgeous man is leaning indolently against it, watching us with fascinated interest.

"Oh, sorry, did we interrupt a party?" I look down at the wooden floors and the puddle we are making. "We won't be long if we could just grab a towel and use your phone."

He shakes his head. "No, no, it's no problem, but I'm afraid the phone is out. The storm must have knocked it out." He purses his lips and shrugs. "But it should be fixed by morning. How about you stay and play, and then in the morning, we can get you some help for your car."

"Xane, was that the Jelliad delegation? Our guests are getting impatient," a musical voice calls from above us. The three of us whirl to face the stairs. Standing at the top is a woman dressed in a French maid's outfit, but it's like one you find at the adult shop, not necessarily one you'd see domestic help wearing. It's short and tight, and she's holding a feather duster in one hand. Her hair is a mess of riotous red curls that are redder than anything I've ever seen before.

She sees us and does a double take. "Oh!"

"Yes, Crimson, not the Jelliad delegation, but two stranded, drenched humans, Susie and Mark! Their car broke down, and they wanted to use the phone. I explained that it is currently out of service." Xane sounds amused as we watch Crimson sashay down the steps like a beauty queen. When she reaches us, she towers over me, almost as tall as Xane and Mark in her high heels.

"Oh no, look at you, poor lambs, all wet from the storm." Her eyes run the lengths of our bodies. Our clothes are plastered to us, and Mark's white polo is see through, highlighting how well he looks after himself. There's no hiding the interest in her eyes. Her nostrils flare, and she zeros in on the cut on my head. "Not only soaked, but injured too. Oh dear. Xane, have you not offered them hospitality?"

she scolds the other man who continues to look amused.

"Oh, I assure you, I have. I was just about to suggest that they remove their sodden clothes so we can find them something more... comfortable to wear before inviting them to join the party."

Before either of us can respond, another voice draws our attention to the top of the stairs—this one husky and annoyed. "Crimson, you dirty skank, you and Xane better not be enjoying yourselves with the Jelliads before our other guests can. The master is about to address the party, and you all need to be in the ballroom."

My eyes widen, and I reach out for Mark's hand as the woman appears at the landing. She also looks like she's raided the adult store costume rack, but her outfit is a deep purple. It looks like it's a bodysuit where all the straps look to be connected. There's a bra section that has straps, but there's only a small scrap of lace material across both nipples. Then there are two horizontal straps across her stomach and waist, both with bows in the middle, and they connect vertically with a pair of lace panties. On top, she wears a sheer, sparkly purple robe that just goes to the tops of her thighs, and on her feet are high heels with fluffy feathers.

Her long blonde hair is in a similar mess of curls like Crimson's, and she has bright silver contact lenses in her eyes.

"Holy shit," Mark mutters, and I don't blame

him. All three of them are fucking delicious, and I have a funny feeling that maybe this place may be more than just a basic bed-and-breakfast.

She stomps down the stairs, smacking the whip in her hand against her other palm. It's not until she's almost at the bottom that she looks up and her mouth rounds in surprise.

"Oh. Not the Jelliads."

I shake my head, getting a little annoyed at the same thing being repeated over and over again while I drip water onto the floor and shiver as blood runs down my face. "Nope, we've definitely established we're not the Jelliads. I'm Susie and that's Mark, and we would definitely like to take you up on your offer of a change of clothes and a bed for the night. If you point us in the right direction, we can get out of your hair."

"Ah, yes, it sounds like you might be busy, so don't let us keep you." My boyfriend peels his eyes away from the beautiful people in front of us and looks down at me, smiling. "And if you have a first aid kit, I can see what I can do about Susie's injury."

Crimson and the blonde move over to Xane, and the three of them have a whispered conversation, one too quiet for our ears, but I really don't care anymore. I'm tired, hurt, and wet, and getting more pissed off as the seconds pass.

Finally, they break apart, all smiles. "Crimson and Savannah will help you out of those wet clothes and into something a little more… comfortable." Xane winks at us, smiling widely. "I'll go see what rooms we have available for you tonight. If you feel up to it, please join our guests in the ballroom for some light refreshments and entertainment. We do want everyone to enjoy themselves when they are at the Pleasure Inn." Xane hurries off, his tails streaming out behind him.

"Come on, let's get you poor lambies out of these wet clothes." Crimson tucks her arm into mine as Savannah does the same to Mark.

They lead us through the house, in the opposite direction of the way Xane went. I marvel as I take in the decor. There are animal skin rugs and a suit of armor, as well as lush, velvety window coverings and wicked, wrought iron, medieval-style furniture pieces. It's a mishmash that really shouldn't go well together, but it does. It gives a warm, inviting, sexy kind of feel to the house.

I can hear Savannah ask Mark what happened, and he tells her the story of our car losing control. She looks back over her shoulder, and I flinch when her overly bright eyes meet mine, but she surveys the cut on my head in sympathy before looking at Crimson again, her eyes narrowing. "Oh, you poor thing. We need to get that bleeding stopped."

I can feel it trickle down my face again now that I'm warming up and we're no longer out in the rain. She stops at a door and reaches for the handle, pushing it open.

"Just through here, you can take off those wet clothes and warm up. Crimson can help Susie with the cut on her face. Let's just say she's a real whiz with blood. I'm sure it's not as bad as it first looked. Cuts on the head always bleed so badly."

"Oh, that's okay, Mark can help me, he's a doctor." Both girls' eyes widen at that bit of information, and they look at him with a little more interest.

"A doctor you say? Well, the master will be interested to hear that. They have been wanting a second opinion on something medically for a while now. Oh, Mark and Susie, your arrival may be the best thing that has happened to us," Savannah gushes, and Crimson bounces excitedly next to me before kissing me on the cheek.

"Oh, Susie, you are like a gift from above. Come on." Crimson drags me through the door, and all I can do is keep up and hope I don't stumble.

I look behind to make sure Mark and Savannah are with us. When I see that they are, and Mark's eyes widen in surprise, I turn forward to see where they have taken us. I feel my mouth drop open in shock. I thought they'd just take us to a bedroom so we could get changed, but it's like we've stepped back in time and entered what looks like a Turkish bath. The room is filled with steam, and there's a large central pool surrounded by rectangular, tiled benches wide enough for three or four bodies to lie on. Arched alcoves line the perimeter of the circular room, and in each of these alcoves is a bubbling hot tub.

"Come, come, let's get you warmed up." Crimson gestures to a door at the side of the room. "The sauna will help with that. Now strip."

CHAPTER THREE

Xane

I leave the humans behind in the capable, if somewhat slutty, hands of Crimson and Savannah and hurry to the office in the back of the house. Unlike a normal Earth office, this one has a high-tech holo screen.

I quickly dial my cousin and tap my finger against the desk as I wait for him to respond.

There's something about our surprise guests that's throwing me off. Humans have very bland emotions and are usually completely emotionally stunted, so much so there is nothing for a warlock to feed off of even if we wanted to. These two, though, are quite the opposite. I can practically see the emotions floating around them, teasing me and inviting me to partake in them. It's an effort in self-control to not partake of what is freely being offered because they have no clue that they are, and neither do I.

Xavier finally answers, but when he does, his face, surprisingly unshrouded, only appears briefly before it's gone. I hear shouts and growls in the background. "What is it, Xane? I'm in the middle of something," Xavier snaps tersely.

My eyes widen as a scuffle appears on the screen. It's my cousin and a kraken shifter, and they appear to be trying to restrain a blood frenzied Vilaxian.

"I'll make it quick, since you seem to be busy," I tell him, and he snorts.

"You think?"

"Two humans just arrived on the doorstep of the Pleasure Inn. They managed to get through the gate, and the female has a hint of warlock manipulation in her. Your signature."

This gets Xavier's attention, and he stiffens, looking off to the side before returning his gaze to me. "Are they okay?" He lowers his voice despite still wrestling with the enraged vampire. Luckily, the kraken has him tangled up in his tentacles for now.

"They seem to have had a car accident, and the female is injured, but not badly. I instructed Crimson to seal the wound," I share, and I see him cringe. He gets shoved out of the way, and a woman appears in the middle of the screen, her eyes narrowed on me. The view is only from the waist up, but I can tell this woman has a banging body.

"Who are you and what have you done with my best friend?" she demands, and I shrug.

"Nothing… yet!"

"Fuck!" my cousin shouts, and all of a sudden, the room is silent. He appears next to the now frozen female, breathing heavily and pushing his long, disheveled hair out of his face.

I grin at him. "Well, cousin, you look to be having fun." I lean back against the desk behind me and study the gorgeous female next to him. "Who's the chick? Have you fucked her?"

Instead of the scoff and eye roll I assumed would come from him—I mean, he is the crown prince of warlocks, and he wouldn't stoop to fucking humans—he growls and his eyes flash sinisterly. "Do not talk about my intimate like she is a piece of meat."

Holy fuck! That gets my attention, and I straighten. "Your intimate is a human? How the fuck did that happen? She won't be able to sustain you. You must be wrong."

He bares his teeth at me, and I shrink back. "Not human. She's Skarrian. The Adams brothers' granddaughter."

"Wow, okay." Before I can probe further, he waves his hand at me.

"I don't have time for this. Take care of Lila's friends."

"When you say take care of them, do you mean patch them up, fog their memories, and send them on their way?" I ask just to make sure, and he frowns.

"Has Aura met them yet?" He strokes the hair on his pretty intimate's head, and I almost gasp at the tenderness, but I slap a hand over my mouth and pretend to cough instead.

"No, they haven't, but I can guarantee they will find both of them tasty morsels. I know I do. They were projecting such strong feelings when they arrived, and I can only imagine how delicious they would taste with the right… motivation."

He sighs and releases Lila from the spell. She jolts with the abrupt change, but then she scowls at him. "Did you cut me off mid-rant?" The woman stares down one of the most powerful beings in the universe without a sense of self-preservation, but all my cousin does is pull her into his arms and coos at her.

"Dude, did you give her your balls?" I joke, and she whirls on me, her green eyes flashing, and I flinch. Xavier just smirks at me and shrugs, but he interrupts her before she can start reaming my ass.

"Lila, honey, this is my cousin, Xane. He resides at the 'bed-and-breakfast' Susie was telling you about." He does bed-and-breakfast in finger quotes, and she narrows her eyes at him.

"Not a B and B?" she asks, and he shakes his head.

"No, it's an alien brothel. A lot of the aliens that use Earth as a holiday destination are not compatible with humans. Aura, the brothel's master, keeps a stable of alien sex workers and bots to cater to any need or kink."

"And your cousin is one of these workers?" Lila asks, looking between us with a smirk. I know she's just trying to get a rise out of me, and it works.

I bare my teeth at her. "Certainly not."

Xavier sighs like he has to deal with two unruly toddlers. "Xane is one of the master's... partners, for lack of a better word."

"How shocking, a warlock prince and master," she sneers, and Xavier shakes his head.

"It's not like that. Unlike Earth, where a master or madam is reviled, the title is a revered and coveted spot in the galaxy. Aura is a very powerful person. Sex pays, and it pays well. Look at what everyone has told you about Link."

"Oh, how is the gorgeous doctor? Hmm, now that is a tasty morsel." I lick my lips at the reminder of the heir to Pleasure Bot Industries.

Lila growls at me and bares her teeth before her body shudders. Xavier shoots me a look of death and pulls her into his arms, caressing her. What the fuck is going on? My silent question is quickly answered when a purple and pink tentacle makes its way up his body and caresses him.

"Holy shit, what is she?" I ask, pointing at the tentacle. "That's not a Skarrian thing."

Xavier shoots me another exasperated look. "You

know Skarrians are polyamorous. One of her mates is a kraken shifter, and she's also courting the doc, so maybe keep your goddamn opinions to yourself."

"My apologies, Lila, that was rude of me." I bow slightly, and her body seems to relax again. I see her shudder, and I assume she's changed back.

"Whoa, sorry, that is still something to get used to. It seems I've gotten a tad territorial."

"No, it was my fault entirely," I apologize again and see my cousin smile at me out of the corner of my eye. Right, future warlock queen, so I need to make good.

"Now what about Mark and Susie?" she asks, looking between the two of us.

"If Aura were to claim Mark and Susie as theirs, there would be no reason for them not to know about the circus," Xavier explains, and she frowns.

"Theirs?"

"Aura is a Morpheian. Morpheians are another species that is polyamorous, and you did say that neither of them are straight."

"Why would it matter if Mark was straight?"

I can see the poor thing is a little confused. Weird, Skarrians usually get a good galaxy education. Maybe she's a little stupid. That does not bode well.

Xavier pierces into my brain like a lightning rod, and I shout out in pain. *She only just found out she's Skarrian. She's been living on Earth all her life, you fucking asshole. She knows very little about the galaxy.*

Fuck, I'm sorry. At least I didn't say it out loud. I can't finish this call quickly enough. I haven't ever had to apologize to someone so much.

"Morpheian are shape shifters, and in their blank natural form, they are hermaphrodites. This allows them to take male or female form. Aura's favorite form is also a hermaphrodite, though your friends will probably assume they are either a drag queen or transgender."

"Like your harem member you said was so much fun?" she asks pointedly, and he actually blushes. I have to hide a snort of laughter behind a coughing fit.

"Wow, cousin, maybe you need a drink of water," Xavier says dryly, and I wave a hand.

"No, no, I'm fine, just a few allergies."

"I don't know. I can't make these decisions for them. They need to make it themselves." Lila wrings her hands in agitation, and Xavier cuddles her close.

"I think what Xane is asking is if they can invite them to play and see how they react to everything? None of it will be nonconsensual, and if they are not open to it, Aura would never force the issue. They just like new and interesting things, and Susie and Mark will be a challenge to them. That's all."

"As long as their consent isn't taken away, I

guess there's no harm in inviting them to join in. They can always say no."

"Yes, and we'd muddle their minds again so they wouldn't remember. I can't do what Xavier did and remove the memory, but I can manipulate it so all they will remember is staying overnight until a tow truck arrived," I assure her, and she bites her lip in indecision.

"I'm saying you can try. I really would like them to be protected." She looks like she knows more than she's letting on, and even Xavier looks surprised that she agreed.

A growling sound behind them interrupts the call. "Fuck, I knew it wouldn't hold him long in his state. Got to go, talk soon." Xavier cuts off the call, and I feel a smile creep across my face. Tonight is going to be so much fun. I hope Crimson and Savannah haven't started without me.

I explode my body into mist and drift through the house toward the baths. Seeping under the door, I situate myself in the corner of the room out of the way and observe what our girls are doing to our newest guests.

The room's hot and smells sweet, with the scent of sandlewood and rose as Crimson and Savannah cajole underwear-clad Mark and Susie into one of the bubbling hot tubs to warm up. Once they are up to their neck in bubbles, Savannah holds out a hand.

"Hand them over," she orders the two nervous-looking humans.

They must have discussed it previously, because neither Mark nor Susie argue, they just strip off their wet underwear and hand it over to the waiting Celestian. She giggles with wicked glee and looks up to the corner where I'm hovering. Of course she would notice I am here. I send a caressing wave of energy toward her, and I see her shiver with desire. I can tell the naughty thing wants desperately to play with our unsuspecting guests, but all of that is up to Aura now. They haven't been interested in playing with any others since Savannah was the last to join our circle.

The likelihood that these two humans will pique their interest is slim. There's nothing particularly interesting about them apart from being extremely pretty for Earthlings. They also had a residue of lust clinging to them when they first arrived. I could tell that maybe they had been doing naughty things before the car went off the road. I could also feel the sexual energy drifting around both of them as they studied me when they initially arrived, and subsequently Crimson and Savannah. Neither of them was immune to our attractive forms. Now we have to hope that what is happening at the party allows them to let out their inner sex freak and play.

I watch as she tosses the wet underwear to the side and grabs Mark by the shoulders, encouraging him to lean back in the water, just as Crimson does the same. "Lean back and relax. You're so tight," she coos to Mark and rubs his shoulders.

"Close your eyes." Crimson's words come out with a hint of compulsion, and it's all they need to do as the girls ask. "Savannah and I are going to help you relax. I'm sure you're both sore after your accident."

"This feels amazing." Susie moans, and if I were corporeal, I'm pretty sure my cock would be hard. Her voice is husky and sounds like sex. Now I just need to hear her moaning our names.

"I'm just going to take a look at your cut and clean it up with a cloth so we can see how bad it is," Crimson tells Susie in the same hypnotic tone to keep them relaxed and not quite focused on what she's doing.

I watch as she leans forward and runs her tongue along it, her eyes rolling back with the taste of human blood. Although their blood is usually watery and bland, humans with B- or AB- blood are tasty, so I'm guessing Susie is one of these rare individuals.

When she pulls away, the cut on Susie's head has healed from the venom produced by Crimson's fangs. I make myself coalesce and wave a hand, projecting an illusion of the cut still being there but not nearly as bad as it was. Crimson smiles and nods her thanks.

"How is everything?" I ask, breaking the silence. The two humans in the tub startle. Susie's eyes fly open, and Mark sits upright, but the two girls coo calm words to them again and they slowly relax.

"Everything is amazing," Savannah gushes. "We're just getting them to warm up. Why don't you go and find our guests something more suitable for tonight's theme party?"

"Oh no, we don't need to join the party, we'd be happy if you would just show us to our rooms," Mark argues, but Savannah draws him back against the bath again, and I see her hands sparkle, causing all the tension to drain out of him once more. She winks at me.

Much like warlocks, Celestians are attuned to feelings, and although they don't absorb them like we do, they can manipulate them slightly. She's just helping Mark feel more open to trying new things. I'm sure she and Crimson will swap places soon, and she will do the same for Susie. A tiny pinch of guilt prickles my conscience. I did promise Xavier's intimate that they would have the right to choose, and mostly they will, but I have a feeling they'll need help loosening up.

"What kind of hosts would we be if we didn't include you?" I ask Mark who has the grace to look sheepish when I sound hurt. "Just wait right there. You are in very good hands with the girls. I'll be right back."

I actually don't need to leave to produce something for them to wear, but I don't think they are quite ready to see me conjure something out of thin air, so I hurry to the room we have set aside for guests to use. It's filled to the brim with anything anyone could desire as far as sexy outfits go. Finding something for these two to wear is going to be fun, especially if I get to help remove it later on.

CHAPTER FOUR

Mark

Savannah's hands are soft, tingly, strong, and sensual as she massages out all the tension I'd been carrying since the accident. My eyes widen in panic as I feel my cock start to harden underneath the bubbles at the feel of another woman's hands on me for the first time in a long time. Looking at Susie, I hope she keeps her eyes closed and doesn't realize what is happening. I feel so fucking rotten. It's not that I want to cheat on Susie or anything, but you'd have to be a dead man not to react, especially when all I can see is my girlfriend also being massaged by an extremely attractive woman. Crimson's hands keep drifting lower with every stroke, and soon she is massaging the tension out of Susie's chest region just above her breasts. Susie's moan of enjoyment is enough to make me imagine what it would be like if Crimson did allow her hands to drift lower and massage my girlfriend's tits.

Fuck, I hope Xane hurries up and returns with some clothes for us so I can abandon this bath before Susie is any wiser.

I watch as Crimson's next pass brushes Susie's nipples under the water, and her subsequent moan is one I'm very familiar with. Susie's nipples are really sensitive, but when her eyes pop open and she looks at me with horror, I have to hide my knowing smirk. It seems like my girlfriend may be just as affected as I am by both of these women.

Susie pulls away from Crimson's touch. "I think I'm warm enough now," she says, not looking back at her. She wraps her arms around herself and won't meet my eyes. "I'm ready to get out. Can you pass me a towel?"

"Of course I can." Crimson disappears into another alcove, and I pull away from Savannah and move closer to Susie. I consider attempting to hide my erection, but I want her to know that she doesn't have anything to feel guilty about and that I was also affected by the gorgeous women.

"Hey, are you okay?" I ask her, and she nods but doesn't meet my eyes. She keeps her gaze down on the bubbling water. "Hey, it's okay," I tell her, putting a finger under her chin. "We're only human," I reassure her, and when she finally meets my gaze, I can see the torment she feels. To distract her, I angle her head so I can see what her cut looks like. Surprisingly, there is only a small line where I thought there had been quite a significant gash. "Oh, hey, this isn't as bad as I thought it was. You don't need stitches at all," I state, and I see that she's grateful for the change of subject. She smiles and rests her forehead against mine as we wait for the girls to return with towels.

"What is this place?" she whispers to me as we look around the Turkish bath. "It's like no bed-and-breakfast I've ever heard of before."

I can hear the hint of worry in her voice, so I wrap my arms around her. "I'm not entirely sure it is a bed-and-breakfast, but that's okay. I don't think they mean us any harm."

"So they are not washing us in preparation to eat us?" she says wryly, and I laugh just as both women return with giant, fluffy towels for us.

"No, I don't think so," I reply as I take the one Savannah offers me before she discreetly turns around. Crimson does the same for Susie, and the two of us hop out, drying ourselves off and wrapping the big towels around our bodies.

"Come on, Xane will have found you something to wear by now." Crimson takes Susie by the hand and drags her back out and down a couple of doors to another room.

"This is my favorite part." Savannah claps her hands enthusiastically as we follow them, but then she tips her head to the side like she's thinking.

"Well, not my absolute favorite, but close. It's like wrapping presents for Christmas."

When I enter the room, I almost crash into Susie who has stopped dead just inside the entrance, and when I take a look around, I can see why. It's like a lingerie shop and a sex shop had a baby and it threw up in here. "Holy shit."

"Isn't it fabulous?" The two girls bounce on the spot, and it's obvious where both their outfits for the evening came from.

"Ah, Susie, I think you were right about this not being a B and B," I say quietly out of the side of my mouth as Xane appears from behind some sheer curtains with a flourish and a wicked grin.

"Oh, we are a bed-and-breakfast, but before that, there's a little bondage and debauchery to go along with it. The Pleasure Inn is one of the most exclusive sex clubs on Earth, and you have arrived on a night when the master is releasing some new, fun options for our most valued clients." I swallow the lump that has developed in my throat, and Xane hands us both some scraps of cloth. "Go change behind there." He pushes us in the direction of the gauzy curtains. "Savannah, Crimson, find out what happened to the Jelliad delegation. The master must be getting impatient," he snaps out, and the girls jump to attention before giving him a kiss on the cheek and hurrying off. "I'll return to you momentarily," Xane assures us and follows them out of the room.

"Fuck, Mark, what do we do?" Susie looks around with a glint of panic in her eyes, her breathing a little erratic and her nostrils flaring. I can tell she's about to go into an epic meltdown, and I want to stop that before it can happen. I place the little pile of clothes Xane gave me to the side, and then I grab both of her hands, squeezing them tightly.

"Deep breaths, sweetie, in and out." I take a deep breath in and encourage her to match me, which she does, and soon the air of panic leaves her. "Good, now tell me what you're thinking. If you want nothing to do with this, we will make a mad dash for the front door right now. I'll grab my wallet and keys from the bathroom, and we'll head back to the car." She's nodding along with my words. "Or…" I feel her hands twitch minutely in mine and smother the smirk that wants to cross my mouth. Of course my crazy girl is going to want to hear the alternative option. "Or we can embrace the opportunity that seems to have fallen conveniently in our laps. We were just promising each other we wouldn't be so vanilla, and this place seems to be right up kink alley…" I trail off, unsure if I should say the next words, but fuck it. You only live once, right? "I was watching you in the hot tub. You seemed to enjoy Crimson's hands on you." The panicky look returns, and she tries to splutter out an excuse or an apology, I'm not sure which, so I place a finger over her mouth. "It's okay, babe. It was hot. I would have liked to have seen more."

Her spluttering breaks off, and she cocks her head to the side. "Really?" she asks, sounding skeptical.

I nod quickly. "Yes, babe. I'm a red-blooded male, and girl on girl is sexy as fuck."

Her eyebrows furrow as she thinks. "I kind of like the contrast of blonde, gorgeous Savannah with her hands on you too, if I'm going to be perfectly honest."

"Oh?" I can't deny I'm shocked. I thought that would have upset her.

"Yeah, the contrast of her pale skin against your tan was beautiful. And I can't deny that I would want to see Xane's hands on you too." Her eyes light up with excitement as she thinks more about my proposal. "Let's stay. No matter what happens, you and I are good, right? We're going to embrace whatever and whoever comes at us tonight, yes?" she asks, raising an eyebrow. "Male or female?"

"Yes, because I love you and I know you love me, and whatever happens is purely physical with anyone else, and something we can add to our spank banks for future dirty talk."

Finally, Susie seems to be on the same page as me. It's like all the guilt she felt for enjoying herself has faded, and she's ready to enjoy whatever comes. I can't deny I feel the same way.

"Well, let's get this party started then. I guess we

should find out what Xane gave us to wear, and there's some makeup and hair stuff here, so let's get pretty." Susie pulls away and goes over to a makeup table, which is covered with products, all of them in wrapping. "This is going to be fun."

I pick up the pile of clothes Xane gave me, finally looking at what it is, and I laugh out loud. Susie turns to see what I'm laughing at. She watches with amusement as I drop my robe and pull on the tight white boxer briefs with a red first aid cross on the front of them. Next, I shrug on the white doctor's coat and sling the red stethoscope around my neck before striking a pose. "What do you think, babe? Dr. Love is in the building."

She giggles as her eyes rake over my body. "Damn, I think you're enough to give a woman heart palpitations. Your dick looks fucking huge in those, and it's not even semi hard." She's not wrong, the outline of my package is practically obscene. "Hang on, let me just..." She pumps something into her hands, comes over to me, and rubs a little amount of oil onto my torso. She then wipes her hands off on the towel wrapped around her before reaching for some black eyeliner. She lines my eyes with it before stepping back and looking me over, licking her lips. "Damn, you are a fucking snack. I'm going to have to beat everyone off." She turns around and does something to her own face as I take a seat on one of the velvet sofas scattered throughout the room.

It takes her about ten minutes to apply some makeup and fiddle with her hair. Her brown corkscrew curls bounce perfectly when she's done, and her chocolatey skin has an ethereal glow to it. She's grinning like a loon when she drops her towel and pulls on her own outfit. I'm not sure how he knew, but hers matches mine, and it's a naughty nurse's outfit. The tight dress hugs her curves and finishes just below the panty line, and it has a V-neck so deep, her breasts are almost spilling out. It has the red cross over one boob and some red piping accents. She settles a little white hat onto her hair that has a red cross on it as well. Bending over, she pulls on a garter belt, followed by some white stockings which she attaches to the belt. I raise my eyebrows at the fact that there is no underwear included, but then my cock starts to get hard at the thought that if she bends over in the smallest amount, her pussy will be on display for anyone to see. I grab hold of my dick, giving it a squeeze as she slips into some red high heels and pulls on long, red satin gloves.

"What do you think?" she asks.

"I think you can get over here and sit on my face," I growl, reaching for her.

"No time for that." Xane appears around the gauzy curtains and looks over the two of us with a critical purse to his plush lips. "Oh my." He snaps a hand to his chest and just about swoons. "You two are going to be a hit. Now come on. We've got places to be." He holds back the curtains and gestures for us to follow him. He turns in a whirl of tuxedo tails and struts out of the room, not waiting for us to follow. I look down at my feet.

"I have no shoes." I look at Susie, and she shrugs.

"Xane didn't either."

Well, okay then. I grab her hand, and the two of us hurry after him.

CHAPTER FIVE

Crimson

My fangs throb and my mouth waters after closing the wound on Susie's head. There's something about her blood that activates my blood-lust, and I'm horny as fuck while we wait for them to get dressed. I pace back and forth in the hallway, trying to get my agitation under control.

"Hey, what's wrong with you?" Savannah asks, leaning against the wall, a small wrinkle of concern between her eyes as she watches my frustrated movements.

I stop and run my eyes up the length of her body. It's gorgeously presented to perfection tonight, and I just want to use my teeth to unwrap her, but now isn't the time. The master would be upset if I unwrapped their present before it was time. Her body starts to glow under my scrutiny. It's tinted lavender, a sure sign that she's just as horny as me. Celestians glow when their emotions are heightened, and the color depends on the emotion. Her wings are away for now, but I know the exact spot to caress on her body to make them come out. I also know exactly how to stroke them to induce the maximum amount of pleasure. Our girlfriend is so responsive and just a little submissive, which works well with all the other rather dominant personalities in our group.

I stalk toward her and put my arms against the wall, boxing her in. "I just need a little something to take the edge off. That human has me all worked up. I have no idea why," I tell her before taking her mouth with mine. She whimpers as she melts against me, her tongue caressing mine in a way that mimics what I'd like to be doing to her clit, but we have no time for that. The humans will be out any minute now. I slide my hands down her body and push her panties to the side. I can feel how turned on she is as I run my fingers through her folds, and she arches her back.

"Touch me, please!" she mutters, and I slide two fingers into her channel and thumb her clit. She clenches around me, and her quiet sigh of pleasure echoes in my ears.

"Sorry, gorgeous. This will be hard and fast." With that warning, my fangs descend and I strike her neck. They slice through her skin like it's butter, hitting her jugular. Her sweet, effervescent blood starts to flow into my mouth, and I drink furiously as I pump my fingers in and out of her.

She writhes in my arms, the orgasm brought on by my venom riding her hard. Her pussy is hot and wet, and the sounds of my fingers going in and out are obscene as her juices flow freely. The noises from her mouth echo down the hallway. I hear the door behind us open, but I can't bring myself to stop. The humans will only see me nuzzling her neck, they won't know that her blood is flowing into my mouth.

"Oh!" Xane sounds amused as I hear them all stop behind us.

I finally swipe my tongue across the puncture wounds, healing them instantly. My bloodlust is under control for now, even though I didn't get to have an orgasm. It will just make it that much sweeter later. I drift my mouth to hers once more, kissing her in thanks as I slowly remove my fingers from her tight cunt and pull her panties back in place. I'm just about to wipe them on my skirt when a hand stops me.

I pull away from Savannah and blink at Xane. He lifts my hand to his mouth and sticks my two fingers inside, sucking hard on them and causing my own cunt to throb with anticipation. His eyes don't leave mine as he licks and twirls his tongue, making sure to get all of Savannah's juices off me. A low groan behind him has him winking at me cheekily. The air is thick with the smell of the two humans' desire, and I grin at him, not hiding my fangs.

Another gasp tells me that one of them saw, but I bet they allow their human minds to tell them it's a costume. I can't wait until one of them lets me use them on their flesh. I'd like another taste of Susie's blood, and I'm curious if Mark's will be bland and watery or flavorsome like hers.

"Well, it looks like the girls got the party started early. I'm not sure the master will be happy about that. They may want to punish both of you," Xane scolds us playfully as he releases my hand and whirls around in a flourish. "Come along, all of you. The show is about to start." Xane gathers up the two humans and ushers them down the hallway to the ballroom. A low thud of the music can be heard from out here, but mostly the room is soundproof. All of the rooms in the mansion are. It wouldn't do for people to overhear what is happening in some of those rooms.

Xane stops suddenly and cocks his head before nodding to himself. "Crimson, love, there's someone at the door again. I can only hope it's the Jelliad delegation, or tonight's crowd is going to be awfully disappointed. Let's hope they don't riot."

Damn it. I wanted to see the humans' reactions when Xane throws open the doors. I scowl at our lover, but he ignores me. I know we can't blow off the Jelliads, but I'm super tempted.

"Oh, and Crimson, you may want to hurry, I think it will start to rain again very shortly."

Well, fuck, the Jelliads won't be fucking happy if it rains and they get washed away. I walk back the way we came, far enough that they can't see me, and then I use my speed to get to the door in an instant. Opening it wide, I usher the five beings in before it starts raining again. Just in time, too, as there is a loud rumble of thunder followed by another flash of lightning.

"Welcome to the Pleasure Inn," I greet them, not sure whom to address. Jelliads are gelatinous blob-like beings with glowing white eyes in the middle of their purple, jelly blob bodies. They have the ability to mold themselves into most shapes, but they are always the same purple-colored, jelly-like consistency.

We are most pleased to be here. One of the creatures starts to glow as they communicate with me tele-pathically. *We were very pleased to receive the master's invite and are very interested in the offer they made us. The five of us are here to see if we can come to a more permanent arrangement.*

The Jelliads don't have names, they have no need for them. They can tell who someone is by brushing their mind, and they don't care if you know who they are or not. They are also not techni-cally allowed on Earth because they have no way of glamouring. I don't even think Xane, who is a powerful warlock, could glamour them enough to pass as human, but they have a skillset the master is very keen on offering as a service for their clients. How the master managed to smuggle them to the planet, I have no idea. The Galaxy Circus is the only legal way on and off this rock. Maybe one day they will share their secrets, but for now, they guard them like nebulas dust.

"Fabulous, we are so excited to have you, and our guests this evening are practically frothing with anticipation. Shall I show you the way?" I gesture for them to follow me and start the trek back to the ballroom, their gelatinous bodies undulating after me.

The sounds of their movements are somewhat similar to what Savannah sounds like after she's been railed by Xane and the master. I skip impatiently, dying to see the reactions from all of our patrons, but then I freeze on the spot. Fuck, the humans. There's no way to glamour them, and I'm not sure we can pass them off as an elaborate costume.

Down the hallway, I can hear the familiar sounds of "Time Warp," and I feel a grin spread across my face. Our patrons do love a good group dance. Humans are such fun when they make up things that even the most uncoordinated being can dance to. Sure enough, when I arrive at the double doors to the ballroom, the whole crowd is jumping to the left and stepping to the right. Susie and Mark have been dragged in, and both are doing the Time

Warp like pros, singing along with the crowd. I catch Xane's eye and wave him over. The Jelliads are just slightly out of view, and I wave my hand at them.

"Can you glamour them?" I ask him, and he grimaces and shakes his head.

"No, due to their nature, glamour doesn't stick. That's why they have never been able to be Earth-side before. I don't even think Xavier, Uncle Cronus, or Aunt Xylene would be able to glamour them. Magic tends to bounce off them."

"Well, what are we going to do about the humans? There's no way they are stupid enough to believe that's a costume." We turn around to look at the Jelliad delegation. The lights from the ballroom bounce off their gelatinous purple bodies, giving them a shimmery glitter effect that's kind of pretty.

"Okay, I'm going to tell them the smoke is laced with erotic, hallucinogenic properties and not to freak out if they see or feel weird things. I'm pretty sure the Jelliads secrete something like that anyway. It's how they can convince someone to feed them."

The warlock is correct. The voice brushes my mind, and from Xane's flinch, I'm assuming he heard it too. A wispy smoke starts to creep out from underneath their forms to create a fog across the ground, which then travels into the ballroom. Xane zips back to Susie and Mark who are having a blast dancing, throwing their arms around and shimmying to the music. My sensitive hearing picks up their conversation.

"I'm afraid I forgot to warn you about the smoke. It has a slight hallucinogenic quality to it. It lowers the inhibitions of our clients so they can really enjoy themselves. It can also make you see things that aren't really there—a little like an acid trip. If you don't want that, I will need to show you both to your bedrooms now."

Susie bites her lip and looks at Mark. Both of their heart rates are elevated due to dancing, so I can't tell how they feel about it either way.

Mark frowns. "Is it dangerous? Could we have a bad reaction?"

Xane shrugs. "There's always a chance but a very small one. Have you done ecstasy before or any other kind of drug?"

Susie nods, her adorable corkscrew curls bouncing enthusiastically.

Mark shakes his head. "No, nothing stronger than weed."

"Hey, remember we promised each other we're all in. Anything goes tonight, and we'll worry about the consequences tomorrow." Susie puts a gentle hand on her boyfriend and squeezes reassuringly.

"The smoke doesn't affect any of us, so we'll make sure you guys are okay, I promise. We'll take very good care of you." Savannah joins them, her angelic light brushing over Mark as she rubs a hand along his back, taking away his more immediate concerns, and I see the tension drain out of him.

"Well, I guess we're staying then," he agrees, and Xane smiles wickedly while Savannah claps her hands.

Before anyone else can say anything, the music cuts off, and the room darkens as a spotlight appears in the center of the stage at the end of the ballroom. The crowd gasps and runs forward, the air ripe with suspense. The master always aims to impress.

More smoke wafts onto the stage, and a swing drops down from above with the master perched delicately on it, their legs crossed and a cape wrapped around them. They are smiling like the cat that got the canary, their long eyelashes closed and their smoky, glitter-covered eyelids sparkling in the spotlight.

When the swing comes to a stop, their feet just hovering over the top of the stage, the master's eyes pop open, showing their bright green cat eye pupils. I hear Susie gasp and feel a smile creep across my lips. Tonight is going to be so much fun.

Master throws back their cape in a flourish and jumps off the swing, striking a pose. "Welcome to the Pleasure Inn and a night none of you will ever forget."

The crowd bursts into applause, and I know it's time to take the Jelliads down into the playroom dungeon. I usher them to the elevator at the side of the ballroom hidden behind another wall. I press the button, calling it to me, and when it arrives and the door opens, I gesture for them to enter, but they are so wide only one of them will fit at a time.

"Shit, we're going to have to do a couple trips," I tell them.

No, we won't. The voice that brushes my mind sounds amused. As one, the five beings all shrink inward and upward, so instead of giant blobs of jelly, they are now long, skinny straws of it. They move forward—don't ask me how, because I'm clueless—until all five fit inside. They shuffle back enough for me, so I follow them in and press the button to descend into the master's dungeon.

CHAPTER SIX

Susie

I can't believe what we walk into once we leave the dressing room with Xane. Crimson has Savannah up against a wall and is finger banging her where anyone could see. I gasp in surprise before I can stop it, and I see Mark closing his doctor's jacket and buttoning one of the buttons to hide his growing arousal. Then I need to stifle a groan when Xane cleans off her fingers. Fuck me, that was hot.

He sends Crimson off to meet someone. How he heard the doorbell, I have no idea, because I didn't hear a thing.

I grab Mark's hand as we follow the other two, and he gives me a reassuring squeeze. Although I'm excited, I'm a little worried we've bitten off more than we can chew, but I'm eager to push my limits.

I've been to a sex club before, but I mostly just watched. The guy I was with wasn't really interested in sharing things with me, more concerned with who else he could fuck for the night. Suffice it to say, that relationship went no further, though that's when I discovered I was into girls just as much as I was into guys.

Xane stops in front of a set of double doors. A low, throbbing sound can be heard, but apart from that, it seems like the room must be mostly soundproof. He throws open the doors with a flourish, and I step back in shock. The room is full of people dancing to a sexy beat, but it's what they are all wearing that has me transfixed.

Each and every one of them has an otherworldly look. I can see fangs, fur, claws, horns, and even tails and tentacles and skin painted in all different colors, with some fantastic prosthetics. Everywhere I look are creatures straight from a science fiction movie or a paranormal romance. Glowing eyes and other naked body parts flash as the crowd writhes to the sensual beat. I'm not sure where to look first, but I strain my eyes to take everything in. Over on one side, I see a woman with her head thrown back in ecstasy while she looks to be impaled on a tentacle thicker than my arm. Shit, I want to know which adult shop sells something like that. It looks to be part of another person's costume. How he can get it to move like that is amazing.

I drag my eyes away from them and watch a green-skinned woman with horns and only one eye get hauled into the arms of a man covered in fur. I can't see what happens, but she throws her head back as he thrusts his hips into her, so I assume he impaled her on his cock. Just as I'm about to look away, I watch another creature join them. This one has scales and translucent wings that flutter behind him. His mask looks like the head of a fly with big eyes and a long protuberance where the mouth should be. My eyes widen as he joins the couple and shoves his long protuberance between them. The woman's mouth drops open, and she screams. I'm not sure if it's in pleasure or agony, but she wraps her arms around its head as if to keep them there, so I'm assuming whatever is going on feels pretty good.

Xane steps into the room, and Mark and I hurry to follow him. Almost as one, the crowd stops moving and turns to look at us, even all the ones locked in erotic bliss, and I shift a little closer to my boyfriend.

"We have some unexpected guests," Xane announces as the music suddenly cuts off. "Please make them feel welcome."

"I think this calls for a group dance," Savannah suggests as everyone continues to stare at us.

"Oh, yes, that would be marvelous." Xane claps his hands, and the familiar sounds of the "Time

Warp" from *The Rocky Horror Picture Show* begin to pump through the room.

The crowd breaks apart and starts cheering as they begin to sing. Even the ones who were fucking seemed to have given that up for now. It's such a change of pace that it's jarring. Mark and I just stand there and watch as Xane and Savannah join the crowd, jumping around and singing. When they get to the familiar chorus, they have basically worked themselves into lines facing us, and they all follow the instructions of the lyrics. I feel myself humming along to it. I do love *The Rocky Horror Picture Show* and had an awful crush on Dr. Frank-N-Furter. He was sexy as fuck.

"I love this movie. Do you know it?" I ask Mark, not remembering if we had talked about it.

"Yeah I do. I dragged my ex to a midnight screening of it once. He hated it, thought it was stupid. Should have known then it wouldn't work."

"Come on." Savannah leaves the group and grabs us both by a hand, dragging us back into the fray. We both allow the gorgeous woman to tug us over, and I take a spot in a line. Mark is farther down, and I'm between Xane and another man who grins at me. His fangs look so realistic in this light, but I get distracted as the song returns to the chorus and I jump to the left with everyone.

There's a huge smile on my face, and I'm breathless as the song comes to a finish. I look around for Mark and find him just as the music picks up again, returning to the same style as before. The crowd starts to writhe in time with the beat, and I want to grab Mark and grind on him for a little while, but the room starts to fill with smoke. My heart races in panic, but it doesn't smell like a fire. In fact, it has a sweet, strawberry scent to it, so I assume it's just dance fog.

A hand on my arm has me jumping, but it's just Mark. He smiles as he starts to pull me into his arms, but Xane is suddenly there. He just keeps appearing out of nowhere. I gasp in surprise, but he just grins. He explains about the smoke, and how it will lower inhibitions and possibly cause hallucinations. Mark voices his concerns, but Savannah joins us, assuring us they'll look after us, and I can see his tension drain away at her reassurance. Normally I'd probably feel pretty jealous of that, but weirdly I don't, I just feel turned on. Maybe the smoke is working on me already.

Once again, the music cuts off, and a spotlight appears on the stage at the front of the ballroom. The crowd falls into utter silence, the atmosphere becoming even more electrically charged as we wait to see what is about to happen.

"Oh goody, here comes the master." Savannah wiggles with excitement and grabs Mark and me by the hand, towing us forward until we are flush against the back of the gathered crowd. I stand on my tiptoes and try to peer around the person in front of me, but they are really freaking tall, and their costume is shaggy, like a Wookiee from *Star Wars*. I feel something brush against the outside of my leg, and when I look down, a tail is brushing back and forth, kind of like a dog's wagging with excitement. Wow, now that is some costume.

A pair of hands land on my waist, dragging my attention away from the Wookiee/dog and to the person whom they belong to. I turn my head and find Xane smiling down at me. In this light, his skin shimmers and almost looks like it's lavender in color. He moves me over and slides me in front of Mark so Savannah and I have the two of them in at our backs and I can see the stage better than before. I look around for Crimson, but I can't see her. She probably hasn't returned yet.

"Pay attention, poppet, you don't want to miss this." Xane's words caress my ear, and his hands, which are still on my waist, tighten in excitement.

A swing drops down into the spotlight, illuminating a figure draped in a cape. He… She… They throw the cape back with a flourish and leap off the swing, throwing their arms wide. "Welcome to the Pleasure Inn and a night none of you will ever forget."

Their voice is a sexy, husky rasp as they strike a pose so we can take in their magnificence, because that's exactly what they are, utterly magnificent. They are tall, with long legs encased in fishnet stockings, and their body is sheathed in a pair of sparkling black booty shorts that do nothing to hide the impressive male package that lies beneath. I can also see an impressive set of washboard abs on a lean waist. As my eyes drift higher, I feel them widen in surprise. They are wearing a sparkly, purple corset covering an impressive pair of breasts. I was not expecting that, but I'm liking it a lot. Their arms are slender and toned, and they have a long neck that makes way for a face that could stop traffic. Pouty red lips glisten in the light, and their eyes are embellished with sparkly red eyeshadow, deep black lashes, and black liner. Their hair is a warm mahogany brown, with loose curls bouncing over their forehead.

"Thank you, thank you." They blow kisses to their adoring public, the crowd clapping and hooting madly with excitement. "Oh, my darlings, tonight is going to be amazing. I'd like to invite you all down to the dungeon for our special entertainment. But beware, if voyeurism isn't your thing, maybe stay up here or continue to one of our many themed rooms for some fun and games." They wink suggestively and have barely taken another breath before the crowd is hurrying to one side of the room in a stampede. "Oh, do be careful and don't panic. I will wait for you to join us. We won't start without you."

"Where are they all going?" Mark asks from behind me, and Savannah giggles musically.

"The elevators down to the dungeon are behind that wall. It's going to be madness for a while."

Just the four of us are left now, since literally everyone else is crowding the side of the room with the elevators. I feel Xane's hands tighten on my waist once more, and when I look back to the stage, I gasp in surprise. The master is no longer up there, instead they have climbed off and are now stalking toward us with a wicked grin.

"My loves." They throw their arms wide as they get to us. "Who do you have here?" They strut around us in a circle, their heels clicking on the wooden floor as they take in Mark and me. "These two don't look like our normal clientele, but their costumes are kind of groovy." They come to a stop behind Savannah and drape a hand around her waist, pulling her into their chest. Savannah's eyes roll slightly as she sags against them and snuggles in.

Xane leans over me, removing his hands, and presses a kiss to the master's lips. They sigh with pleasure as he pulls away. "You look gorgeous as usual," Xane tells them, and they pat him on the cheek.

"Oh, you do know how to woo a gal. Now be a dear and introduce us." They wave their hands at the two of us.

"Master Aura Gasm, it is my pleasure to introduce you to Mark and Susie. They were on their way back from Vegas when they had a little car trouble. They were hoping to use our phone to call for help. Unfortunately, a tree has knocked out the line, so I invited them to stay and attend our little party."

The master stares at Xane a moment longer before their gaze turns to us. "Enchanté." They hold out their hand, and Mark takes it and places a kiss on the back.

"Thank you for having us, Master Gasm," he says politely. "We're sorry to be a bother."

"Nonsense, and please call me Aura. I'm just a little surprised you got through the gate. I thought it had been locked for the evening with the storm and all." They turn their attention to me, and when I see their tongue poke out and wet their lips, I just about groan out loud. "Well, aren't you a tasty little morsel?" They let go of Savannah and step around her, holding out their hand once more.

I take it and lift it to kiss the back much like Mark did, but instead they pull me in and dip me, placing a kiss on my lips. Savannah giggles as they put me back on my feet and wink.

"Pleased to meet you, both of you. Very pleased indeed." They reach down and adjust their bulge inside their pants. "Now, would you like to accompany us down to the playroom? We have such wonderful things to explore." They turn around and saunter back toward the stage.

Mark looks over to the large crowd still trying to use the elevators. "Might be waiting a while."

"Ha, we won't be using that one, it only goes to the viewing platform. Come on, the master has their own private one." Xane puts his hand on my back, and Savannah grabs Mark by the hand, before they lead us after Aura. I'm in a little bit of a daze, confused and horny all at the same time. I'm guessing the smoke is starting to have an effect on me. It still drifts across the floor despite most of the crowd leaving the ballroom. It kicks up with every step we take. Xane's fingers caress my back in a gentle circular motion, and I look up at him. He winks and gives me a reassuring nod as we arrive at an old, metal gated elevator. Master has already stepped into it, and Savannah drags Mark in after them.

Aura spins Mark around and pulls him closer. They run their hand down Mark's coat and pop the button open. "Now that's more like it," they say, pushing it back on his shoulders a bit to expose his toned chest. "If all doctors looked like this, well, I'd probably hurt myself more often," they mutter, stepping back slightly and giving Mark some room.

"And he's a real one too." Savannah plays with the stethoscope around Mark's neck, licking the bit that is supposed to go against the body, and he looks at me with wide eyes. I have to smother the smile that threatens to cross my lips at his panic, but before I can say anything, the master raises an eyebrow.

"Oh really? Well that is interesting. After we've played, I may have a patient for you if you're interested."

Mark stutters a little, but he finally regains some of his sense, and I see the confidence I know is there come to the surface. "Of course, Master, I am at your service."

"Oh, damn," Xane mutters behind me when the master's eyes shine with delight. "You two are done for now." He gives me a gentle nudge, and we step onto the elevator, then Xane pulls the metal gates closed behind us.

CHAPTER SEVEN

Aura

Imagine my surprise when I notice two humans in our midst—one who has very recently been touched by warlock magic not of my own warlock's hands. Instead of kicking them out and muddling their minds like I should, I invite them to stay and join in the fun. It might have something to do with the fact that they are both totally fuckable, but they also have a strange draw to them, something I've never felt from any other human I've come in contact with.

As the elevator journeys downward, both of them fidget with nerves, but Xane quickly distracts me with pertinent information.

The warlock magic on her belongs to my cousin Xavier.

Ah, the warlock princeling. No wonder it is

potent. I knew the circus was recently on Earth, but I hadn't realized they were close by.

Susie is his new intimate's best friend. Lila is the Adams brothers' granddaughter who has recently been found living on Earth. She received permission from the Adams brothers to tell her all about the circus and gave her the choice to remember or have her mind wiped. She chose to forget so that no one could use them for the information.

The Adams brothers are quite delicious, and I may have tried to seduce them at one point, but they are still completely devoted to their missing mate despite how many years she's been missing. So instead, we are friends, and I respect them immensely. I hadn't heard they had a granddaughter. I knew they were devastated when they lost their son and his mate, and I thought the child had been lost too.

I look at the two humans with a new eye. I respect her decision to forget to protect their friend, but it's not just the warlock magic drawing my attention, and the man practically sparkles with vitality too.

There's something else about them. I can't quite put my finger on it, but they call to me, I muse, and his eyes widen in surprise.

I feel it too. Their emotions are delicious and big, like nothing I've ever felt from a human before, let alone tasted, but it's there right in front of me, just waiting for me to reach out and take it all for myself. He sounds confused, and that makes me smile with delight. Not much rattles my warlock lover, so it's fun to see.

The elevator comes to a stop before we can continue our conversation. Xane and Savannah assist the two humans off, and I almost wish I was in front so I could see their reaction to my favorite room in the building.

We only open it for clients to play in once a week. Mostly they use my employees' individual bedrooms for their transactions, which all have fun things in them too, but so many species in the galaxy get off on feeding from energy or from voyeurism that it would be neglectful of me not to have a sex dungeon for them to partake in.

I can tell the moment the humans realize where we are. I hear both of their heartbeats jump in their chests—nervousness and excitement, I'm sure. Pushing past them, I stroll out into the middle of the viewing area. I have all sorts of swings and benches and delightful mechanical things for people to be thoroughly fucked on down here. Looking up into the viewing gallery, I smile at the waiting guests, their loud, excited chatter drowning out the music playing down here, while my employees are busy making sure that our guests' whims and needs are seen to.

Savannah and Xane have corralled the humans off to the side, and Crimson has the Jelliads stationed around the room. At the moment, they look like giant Jello statues. The excited noise drops off momentarily as my guests take in the new additions to the room, but the noise quickly picks up again as they realize who and what they are. I wonder what the humans are making of all this. Earlier, the way all of my customers look could have easily been written off as costumes, but once they get a closer look at what's about to happen, there is no way they are going to be able to play it off like that.

"Friends and valued clients, you are all here today for a special treat. I have managed to smuggle some Jelliads onto the planet for us to have a little bit of fun with."

The crowd's cheers echo around the room.

"My gorgeous assistant, Buttercup, and her sexy helpers, Buzz and Woody, will be in charge of who is next in line." Three of my fellow Morpheians appear at the front of the railing in their chosen forms for tonight and wave to the crowd. "They have a list of who signed up and paid first—and people who are on time will get rewarded—so please be kind to them. People who do not obey the rules will be evicted and banned." I growl the last bit, and the noise dies down once more as two of my Bacaclian security step up next to Buttercup. Their bright red, armor-plated bodies are on high alert, their pincers clicking menacingly as the crowd steps back slightly. One swings a stalked eyeball in my direction and winks before returning to the crowd.

I wave my goodbye and return my interest to my two humans. "Well, darlings, step right this way. As our very special guests, you get to play in one of these first." Crimson, Xane, and Savannah escort them over to the closest Jelliad. At the moment, their eyes are powered down and they truly look like big blobs of Jello.

"What is this?" Susie asks, definitely wary of what is going on.

"Much like the smoke above, these… blobs have a certain property to them. Once you step in, they act very much like ecstasy, giving you a rush of good vibes and, well, horniness. They have stimulating properties, and they really are a lot of fun," Xane explains, putting it in terms they will understand.

"So we're going to want to fuck?" Mark says dryly, and my lips turn up.

Xane shrugs sheepishly. "Yup."

They exchange a glance with one another, and the four of us hold our breaths. This will be the turning point. If they refuse, I'll have one of the girls escort them to a room upstairs and lock them in for the night none the wiser, but if they decide to be daring, then I can say I'm excited to see what happens afterward. It's like they are having a conversation with their eyes. It's telling that they have been a couple for a while, and I get a feeling of warmth and joy about it. That's really freaking weird. Normally I couldn't care less about anyone else other than my three partners. Suspicion starts to build.

I reach my mind out to the Jelliad in front of me, and they respond without opening their eyes.

What is it, Master Gasm? You seem troubled.

Would you please scan these two once they enter you? Normally I wouldn't violate their privacy like that, but both Xane and I are having weird reactions to them.

Crimson did too, Xane tells me. *You should have seen her face when she tasted Susie's blood. It was unlike any reaction to human blood she's had in the past.*

I will tell you what I discover, the Jelliad assures me serenely, already producing the feel-good toxin needed for what is about to happen.

A pang of guilt tickles me, but I quickly brush it away and justify it by reminding myself I'm only protecting my family and livelihood by being well informed. It wouldn't be the first time someone has tried to infiltrate my organization from the inside and destroy it—other jealous galaxy beings wanting a slice of the pie, or human authorities trying to shut me down. There are not many who could get past my warlock, but there's always a first time.

Susie and Mark must come to an agreement, because Susie nods and looks up at me, her long lashes framing her pretty chocolate-colored eyes. When they meet mine, I feel a punch in the gut, and I subconsciously lean toward her as she wets her lips with her pretty pink tongue. "Let's do this."

"Wonderful." I clap my hands, and the girls giggle with excitement as a slow smile creeps across Xane's face. "If you would strip, we can get started."

"Naked?" Mark pauses, and I lift one shoulder.

"Yes, your clothes are only going to get in the way," I explain, and they look around the room at the other four blobs of Jelliad, which now have people surrounding them.

"But they are not taking off their costumes," Susie points out as a fur-clad, wolf-like creature climbs into one of the purple blobs. Instantly, he throws his head back and howls, and we watch as his long, naked cock pushes through his fur as it becomes erect. Another wolf creature climbs in with him and gets on their knees, licking the jutting member with their tongue while avoiding cutting it with their sharp fangs. The first creature leaps at them and throws them around onto their hands and knees, pulls their hips up, and thrusts deep. I turn back to the couple whose mouths are now open in shock.

"Oh, I'm pretty sure they have everything they need," I remark, not wanting to tell them they are as naked as they are going to get.

Susie shrugs and starts taking off her dress, grabbing it by the hem and lifting it over her head. Her gorgeous breasts tumble out, revealing her pretty, dark nipples which are just begging to be sucked on. I feel my own cock harden with excitement as I scan her body, clad only in suspenders and stockings, as she hands the dress to Savannah who can't drag her eyes away either. In fact, Susie has all our attention, including her boyfriend's, whose own cock starts to grow beneath his costume. She puts her hands on her hips, all shyness gone now, the smoke from upstairs doing a good job of lowering her inhibitions.

"Come on, baby. I've been horny. You promised we'd just let go for tonight."

That's when I see Mark make a decision. It's like he finally gave himself permission to let loose. Up until now, he's been holding onto his inhibitions, but as Susie slips off her heels and goes to unclip her stockings, he throws out a hand.

"Can you leave those on?" He looks to me for confirmation, and I smile wickedly.

"Oh, most definitely."

A slow grin creeps across his face as he shrugs out of the doctor's jacket and hands it to Savannah who throws both items behind her, and Crimson takes the stethoscope from around his neck, rubbing her body against his as she does. Naughty vampire. We all wait with bated breath as he tucks his thumbs into the waistband of his briefs before drawing them down his long, toned legs and kicking them to the side. When he stands back up, his cock sticks out, already dripping with precum, and my mouth waters.

I hear Xane groan inside my head. *What a pretty cock.*

He's not wrong. Although it's red and angry, it's thick and long, and I bet it stretches you out wonderfully.

I step up and hold out a hand for each of them. Neither hesitates, and they both take one and allow me to draw them closer to the Jelliad.

"Now, when you get in there, it is a weird feeling. Although you will be surrounded by the… gel, you will still be able to talk and breathe, so don't hold your breath. You'll only find yourself passing out and missing out on all the fun," I warn them as we stop in front of it.

"But how do we get in?" Susie asks, and without answering, I put my hand on her back and shove. She stumbles forward, and with a sucking, squelching sound, enters the Jelliad. I watch as her eyes widen in surprise and her mouth rounds before she quickly clamps it shut, but she must remember my warning, because I see her take a small test breath before relief fills her eyes.

"Do you need a hand too?" I turn, placing my hand on Mark's very firm chest, and I feel it ripple beneath my palm. His nostrils flare as I brush against him, and I know he's not unaffected.

He takes a deep breath and looks me dead in the eye. "Maybe later." One corner of his lips turns up before he takes a deep breath and dives right in with his girlfriend.

I step back and feel my partners gather around me. Crimson snuggles into my side as Savannah does the same for Xane. I watch on with glee as I see the effect of the Jelliad take hold of the two humans in front of me.

"This is going to be fun."

CHAPTER EIGHT

Mark

I was expecting the jelly to be cold and had braced myself for it, but when I dive in, it's warm and comforting and exactly how you'd expect jelly to feel—a little thick and slimy but not altogether unpleasant. Surprisingly, I can breathe even though I'm completely submerged.

I wasn't expecting much when I dived in. I don't know of any substance that can cause the kind of reactions they suggested without ingesting it. Now that I'm in here, though, I find myself growing warm with that tingling feeling of being aroused, and my dick throbs in want. It was already hard seeing Susie strip in front of everyone. Knowing that they were looking at her and admiring her was a big fucking turn-on, and seeing her confidence was the ultimate aphrodisiac, so yeah, I was hard before I even entered the gel, but now it's *more*.

I've never done hard drugs, only a bit of weed during college, my medical degree always stopping me from indulging, but now I'm guessing this is how being on ecstasy must feel. My body tingles all over, and my sexual arousal starts to increase. I look around the gel and reach for Susie. Her pupils are blown, and she has a goofy smile on her face. I drag her toward me through the gel, and she moves easily with only a small amount of resistance. The purple gel coats our skin, and as I pull her flush against me to kiss her, she giggles as we slip and slide against one another.

I wrap my arms around her, and her legs come up and wind around my waist. My throbbing cock is trapped between us, and as we tangle our tongues together, she slides up and down, grinding her clit on it. Our breathing increases, and we're both panting as we pull away. I tear my gaze from her and look at our surroundings. The gel is translucent, but it has a distorted appearance, kind of like looking through a textured window. I can see Aura and the others on the other side, but I can't quite make out expressions or details.

While I'm looking, Susie places tiny, open-mouthed kisses against my chest, still grinding on my length. "Please, Mark, I want you to fuck me hard," she begs breathily, not one bit concerned about where we are or what we're doing.

Without regard for anything or anyone around me, I thrust deep into her hot pussy. It's not an easy slide since I'm big and I haven't done any prep. Her groan is loud in the enclosed space as her pussy grips my dick, fluttering with my forced entry. I retreat and thrust twice before fully seating myself and reveling in the feel of her. Everything is just so much more. Heightened senses and nerves make this encounter unlike anything I've ever experienced before. Her thighs tighten around my waist, and I don't have to worry about holding her up, the gel taking care of it for me. When she nudges her heels against my ass, signaling she's ready, I don't hold back. I fuck into her like I never have before, hard and fast, almost feral in its intensity. She moans and gasps and holds onto my shoulders tightly, her nails leaving little half circles where they dig into my skin.

"Oh my god, yes!" she cries out as I lean in and take a nipple into my mouth. I can't help but ingest some of the gel as I lick and suck her breast all while riding her hard. The gel is somewhat sweet and not unpleasant, and I can feel a rush as I swallow it down, sort of like I'd had ten shots of espresso and tequila at once and my head feels intoxicated.

I bury myself into her soft depths over and over, my actions completely out of control as something takes over my body. The tingling starts in my toes as I feel my impending orgasm start to rise. The wave rushes up my body, tightening my balls, and I squeeze my butt cheeks as I angle her to hit all the right spots inside her.

Her pussy tightens as I slip my hand between us, and all it takes is one slick slide of my thumb across her clit and she detonates like a firework. She throws her head back and clamps her heels down, holding me as I try to thrust through my own orgasm. Her pussy walls tighten, milking me. There's no way I can stop this, so I ride the wave.

My body feels like it's floating, and all of a sudden, the gel starts to glow, and Susie and I are locked in place, our orgasms ongoing as the gel starts to undulate. A low thrumming sound can be heard as the gel ripples and rolls, tossing us around. It stops abruptly, and we're frozen in place. The glow intensifies, and I see Susie's eyes roll back into her head before her body goes limp in my arms. I can't move, still locked in place with whatever is happening. My heart pounds, but it's no longer from the orgasm that just won't stop. I look through the gel, seeing if I can catch anyone's attention. Just outside the gel, closer than they were before, Aura, Xane, Crimson, and Savannah watch on, seemingly riveted to what Susie and I have been doing, but even now that things are happening, none of them are moving. I can't wave, shout, or anything.

Suddenly, the glow intensifies, and my vision is blinded, and then I see nothing but darkness.

Xane

The two humans are beautiful in their passion. Overtaken by the effect of the Jelliads, they fuck like the primal creatures they are—like the primal creatures that surround us. The Earth would be a much better place if it had a regular hit of Jelliad mojo to temper their more prudish ways. The rest of the galaxy is more evolved than that, and although we still go to war against one another over petty squabbles, we tend to be united as planets. Who has time for petty infighting when there are bigger enemies out there? And sex? Sex is seen as a celebration of life by most cultures, though there are still the odd one or two that are set in their own prudish ways.

I pull Savannah in front of me and slide my arms around her body, cupping her breasts and rubbing my throbbing member against her ass. I slide a hand into her skimpy panties and glide my fingers through her soaked lips before dragging the moisture back to her clit. I circle it a couple of times as she rubs back against my cock, groaning her own pleasure as our eyes remain locked on the gorgeous sight in front of us.

"Fuck," Crimson mutters as she bites her lip,

enthralled with the view in front of us. "Mark can really use that cock, can't he?" she says and paws at Aura, who grabs her and spins her so her chest is to their front before pinning her arms behind her body. They lean in and nip a nipple through the maid's dress.

"Behave yourself, my sweet. There will be plenty of time to play. When they finish their session, we will invite them up to my boudoir. I'm sure the rest of our guests can keep the Jelliads sated for the night," Aura playfully scolds our Vilaxian girlfriend.

Just at the moment of climax, something happens, something none of us were expecting. The Jelliad was just supposed to start glowing as it gently absorbed their climax, but instead, it starts vibrating and low-key humming, its body jiggling like it's being rocked by an earthquake.

"What's happening?" Savannah takes the words out of my mouth, and Aura and I exchange a look.

"I asked them to get a read on the two humans, but this is not what I thought would happen." They run a frustrated hand through their soft curls and take a step forward. I'm right there with them.

Suddenly, Mark and Susie are frozen, and I watch as the light and movement intensify. Susie succumbs first, and she passes out. I dive at the jelly mass, trying to get in there and help them, but I smack against a solid surface and bounce back, Aura's hands stopping me from falling on my ass.

"What the fuck?" Crimson tries to use her Vilaxian strength to do the same, but she's also locked out. She bangs on the side of the Jelliad in frustration as we watch Mark also succumb to whatever is happening to them.

"What's going on? We need to help them." I can hear the panic in Savannah's voice, scared about what's happening to the two humans.

How quickly we've become attached.

The light within the Jelliad dims, and the movements settle as they finally open their eyes and look at us. *Calm yourselves.* Their voice has an echoey quality to it, so I know they are talking to all four of us. *The humans are okay, they are just a little overwhelmed with the process, and I'm afraid I disturbed some mind wipes that both of them had been subjected to. All of the memories came flooding back, and it overwhelmed them. Give them a moment to recover. I've flooded my body with healing energy, so it won't be long now.*

"Both of them had their minds wiped?" Aura sounds relieved but also curious, and I don't blame her. Xavier said that he had only wiped Susie's mind, and Mark's had been untouched.

Yes, the male's is very old and deeply rooted. They are both actually fascinating. I do love a good mystery, the Jelliad muses somewhat jovially, and I feel my eyebrows jump in surprise. They are known for being a very sedate, serious race, so to hear any kind of emotion from them is unusual.

"Oh?" I prompt, desperate to learn more.

Hmm, yes. You know that most humans descend from the Skarrian race that crash-landed on Earth so many years ago, and how they lost their powers because they no longer had contact with the magical waters of Skarr, yes?" he asks, and the four of us nod, so it continues. *Well, some of them still contain that internal ball of energy from their power source, and this female has recently come in contact with water from Skarr. Her power source is bubbling just below the surface. Any more of the Skarrian water, and I would say she'd probably develop powers. Oh, and she also remembers everything about her experiences and knowledge about the circus, so I'm sure she will have some questions when she gets out.*

"Well, that is very interesting," Aura muses, bringing their hand up to their chin and rubbing it.

"Xavier did say that his intimate had only just discovered she was Skarrian as well. I'm guessing she had the water on hand to kick-start her own powers. I wonder if all humans would end up with powers if they had access to it."

No, I'm fairly sure it's mostly latent, but this one has been living with the Skarrian granddaughter of the Adams brothers, which would explain why hers is slightly active.

"What about Mark?" Savannah is leaning against the still solid Jelliad, her fingers spread across the surface like she's trying to reach for him. I guess Savannah's connection with Mark goes a little deeper than we thought. A tear runs down her face, and her glow is blue, tinged with brown, showing she is sad and worried.

Don't worry yourself, gentle Celestian, they will both be okay, and there is a reason why you feel so attached to the male. It is somewhat of a conundrum as to how he came to be on Earth. When I scanned his memories, I discovered that he is not of Earth. He thinks he is an orphan and spent his years growing up in foster care, working hard to get his medical degree. He has an affinity for healing due to his race. His very first memories are foggy, so I actually have no idea how he came to be here. I guess only time will tell.

"Well, what is he then?" I ask, getting a little impatient at the Jelliad for drawing this out.

He too is Celestian, which is why young Savannah is having such a strong reaction to him and why he is so skilled with healing. When his power core is activated, he will be able to heal with his will alone, and he will be powerful.

Savannah gasps and puts a hand over her mouth, her eyes wide as she watches the two humans inside the Jelliad.

I would suggest you reach out to the Celestian council. They like to keep track of their flock, and they may know of one who has gone missing just under thirty years ago. I have also imparted all the knowledge of alien races into his brain so that when they emerge, he won't need to be caught up on everything. He now knows what the female does.

Savannah's eyes get wider, and she shakes with emotion as her colors cycle like a mood ring, running the gamut of the rainbow.

"Savannah, honey." Aura holds their hands out toward our pretty angel who throws herself into their arms and starts sobbing. "What do you know?" they ask her carefully, aware that she is all over the place emotionally.

"The royal flock's first-born child was stolen approximately twenty-eight years ago by enemies unknown and has never been seen again. The two queens have been despondent ever since. It's why the council has such power these days. They had to take over because the royal flock was grieving. Only King Jontal continues to be actively involved in the running of our world. That is why there is going to be a vote to abolish the monarchy and become a republic very shortly."

"Well, if that's not fucking suspicious, I have no clue what is. I guess I will be sending a missive to King Jontal as soon as possible." Aura squeezes her tight before wiping her tears away and pressing a gentle kiss to her lips. "But first, I think it's time for these two to know the truth. Can you release them?" they ask the Jelliad, who blinks twice before responding.

They need a few more minutes for their minds and bodies to fully heal. I'm afraid it did more damage than I thought it would, and I want them fully healed before I release them.

"Why doesn't he show any sign of Celestian powers? And he definitely doesn't have wings. Savannah was rubbing his shoulders and back and pressed on the spot that releases their wings involuntarily, but nothing happened." Crimson seems to have recovered quickly, and I see her slice her lip with a fang as she worries on it before raising an eyebrow and crossing her arms. She's getting annoyed at the little bits and pieces, and she wants the full picture so she can assess the danger and respond correctly. It's such a Vilaxian thing to do.

"There's a ceremony when we are six. An object of great power is used to activate our powers. Celestian children would be a nightmare if they had power and wings before that age. By six, they are mature enough to make good decisions and go to school to learn how to control their powers and wings. Mark, whose name is actually Marcus Angelis, wouldn't have had that. No ceremony, powers, or wings."

A groan and movement has us all turning with anticipation. I press my hand against the Jelliad's side, and this time it goes through.

They are ready now, it announces before powering down and allowing the humans to leave its mass.

I reach through and hold out a hand for one of them to grab while Aura does the same for the other. I feel a shiver of anticipation run down my spine. I can't wait for what happens next.

CHAPTER NINE

Susie

I try to roll over, not wanting to drag myself out of my warm bed, but it feels a lot harder than it normally does. In fact, it's like wading through syrup, and it feels like I'm surrounded by it. I feel my eyes pop open and prepare to scream when I see myself covered by a thick, purple, gelatinous substance, but then I remember what happened. Aliens!

Aliens exist, my best friend Lila is one, and now I am trapped inside one of them. I scramble around, looking for Mark, and grab his hand when I find him. He's unconscious, but he has a tiny wrinkle of a frown between his eyebrows.

"Mark," I hiss, trying to get him to wake up. I swim my way over to him, the gel easy to move through once more. I remember everything that happened. The animalistic way Mark fucked me, the never-ending orgasm, the information overload when the gel started glowing, and a voice, a soft, gentle voice assuring me everything was going to be okay. I also remember everything that happened when we went to visit Lila, and now my heart is racing a million miles an hour, and my breath hitches in panic. We are in an alien brothel, but who's to say these are the good guys? Who's to say we're not being tested and trained to become one of the sex workers? A fun, interesting time for an otherworldly creature?

As I squeeze Mark's hand and hiss again, trying to get him to wake, I scan our surroundings. I can just make out the four beings we've had contact with since we've been here. I'm going out on a limb and assuming none of them are human. They are hazy through the gel, but I can see them talking, their mouths moving. Xane and Aura both reach out a hand as if to assist us, and I flinch back. Xane frowns and seems a little hurt, but I don't care. All I care about is getting Mark and myself out of here in one piece.

I hear Mark breathe in deeply and turn to see his eyes open as he sits up from the reclined position he'd been in. "Aliens!" he shouts and looks around frantically. I squeeze his hand again, and his eyes meet mine. He sighs in relief, his gaze softening slightly as the panic recedes slightly, but then he takes in our surroundings. "Fuck, Susie, they're aliens. The circus is all aliens too. I knew those special effects were too good." His words rush out of his mouth, and I nod.

"I know. Lila told me everything, but I chose to have Xavier wipe my mind so that I wouldn't have to lie to you. Why do you think I remember now? And how do you know?" I tip my head to the side. So many questions are running through my brain. My previous panic is dying down, now that Mark is conscious again, and being replaced with the innate knowledge that we're not in any danger. Why am I so calm all of a sudden?

That's because I'm taking away your panic. The voice brushes against my mind, and I see Mark flinch, his hand tight in mine once more, so he must hear it too. Suddenly, two big eyes appear in the gel in front of us.

"Agghhhh!" I can't stop the scream that leaves my mouth, and both Mark and I scramble backwards, trying to find purchase in the gel, but it's slippery and thick, and neither of us get very far.

Calm yourselves. None of us mean you any harm. The voice in my head is serene and soothing, and I feel the tension in my body drain away once more. *If you would allow the master and the warlock to assist you out of my body, they will explain everything to you. I'm afraid I am in need of another meal, and you must allow some other creatures to take your place.*

Meal? What the fuck? Mark and I exchange a

glance, and this time both of us scramble to take the proffered hands, allowing them to pull us through the jelly mass. When my feet hit solid ground again, I expect to have jelly dripping off of me, but to my surprise, I'm completely dry—even the stockings and garter are dry. The only thing that's wet is Mark's cum that is now dribbling down my thighs. I cross my hands over my breasts and pussy, feeling incredibly self-conscious all of a sudden. Whatever drugs that had been flowing through my system from the smoke is now well and truly gone, the creature having stripped that away as well as the block on my memory.

"What the hell is going on?" Mark demands forcefully with his hands on his hips and legs spread like he's waiting for a fight, not self-conscious at all. He crosses his arms, and his muscles ripple. All four of the aliens in front of us zero in on the movement. Xane licks his lips, and I see Crimson's eyes dilate with desire. None of them are doing anything to hide their interest in my boyfriend.

Savannah skips away but quickly returns, holding out fluffy robes to both of us. I take it with a grateful nod to the pretty blonde, who, now that my alien knowledge has returned, I can see glows with an inner light I hadn't noticed before. I'm dying to ask them what they all are, but I'm not sure if that question is a social faux pas or not. Movement behind us has me turning, and my mouth drops open in shock before I can stop it. Climbing into the now vacant jelly mass is a couple of long-limbed creatures. They kind of look like the children's character *Gumby*. All smooth with blue shiny skin and arms and legs with no hands or feet. They have two round eyes and a mouth but no nose and no hair on any parts of their bodies. I also can't make out any distinguishing sex organs. I blink a couple of times, before shaking my head to try and kick start my brain again.

"Seriously, someone better start talking or I'm going to lose my shit," Mark orders once more, and Aura nods and gestures to the side.

"We will explain everything, but we shall do that somewhere less… distracting." They gesture for us to follow them. Crimson and Savannah tuck their arms into Mark's and lead him after the master, Savannah's hands glowing on his arm.

"What is she doing?" I ask when Xane offers me his arm. He looks to where I'm pointing and smiles gently.

"See how her hand is glowing yellow? That means she's only giving him reassuring vibes and easing some of his panic. What color her light glows depends on what vibe she's feeling or bestowing. Mostly, her powers are for good. Celestians don't really have a capacity for evil or bad."

I release the breath I had been holding, and when my gaze drifts back to Xane, I flinch. I hadn't noticed before because of everything else, but Xane looks different now too. His cheekbones are sharper, and his ears have a point to them that they hadn't had before. The biggest difference, though, is the color of his skin. Before, his skin tone was similar to Mark's, but now he's a lilac color, and his tattoo's shimmer a pearlescent white. His hair is still indigo, but it also has a shimmer, almost a glow, to it. It's his eyes that are the most startling. His pupils are bright purple and elongated like a cat's. He looks exotic and different and incredibly sexy. I'm having a visceral reaction to the whole package, and I feel goosebumps break out across my skin. His lips curl up in a secretive grin, and he tucks my hand under his arm before leading me in the direction the others went.

"I'm sure this must be all so confusing for you. You can ask any questions you want, and we will answer honestly."

I shake my head, clearing out the desire that was riding me. "Are you a warlock? One of Lila's partners is a warlock. He's the one who locked my memories away. He promised he would return them next time they came through Earth and that we could tell Mark as well," I tell him as we wind our way down a dimly lit tunnel away from the sex dungeon.

"Yes I am. Xavier is my cousin. Your friend Lila is his intimate. Did they explain that to you?"

"Kind of. Something about being his soulmate."

I'm still a little shaky on everything because she also had Caspian whom she was mated to and Link who she was… dating.

"Yes, I can see how it may be confusing. Each race has their own individual mating customs, and Lila being a Skarrian would make her polyamorous, so she has the potential to mate with many. I will explain about warlocks as best as I can. You are correct, soulmate is probably the most appropriate Earth term for what Lila is to Xav. Most life-forms put off energy in the form of emotions and feelings, and warlocks use these to sustain their powers. The more powerful the warlock, the more people he needs to 'feed' from to stay powerful. It is common for warlocks to have harems. These are groups of people they feed from. And yes, more often than not, this involves a sexual relationship because an orgasm is a powerful feeling. It is a contractual relationship that frequently involves monetary payment, as well as gifts and lodgings. Sometimes it evolves into more, especially if a warlock doesn't find their intimate. An intimate is the warlock's version of a soulmate, able to see to their every need, including providing the warlock with all the power they require so they don't need to feed from anyone else. It is a deep and loving relationship, and something every warlock dreams of. It is also rare. Lila is this to Xavier."

"Have you found your intimate?" I ask, and he shakes his head, a spark of mischief in his eyes.

"No, but I'm not upset. Have you seen who I feed from?" He chuckles. "My relationships with Aura, Crimson, and Savannah are just as committed and loving as an intimate bond without the official ties. None of us have looked anywhere else for sexual company for years now, that is until you two appeared on our doorstep looking cutely bedraggled."

I stop suddenly, forcing Xane to stop as well. "You're interested in us... sexually?"

He grins and bumps my hip with his. "I mean, have you seen the two of you? We'd have to be blind not to see how hot both of you are, and damn, Mark can fuck like an animal. You put on quite a show."

I feel my cheeks heat with embarrassment. Of course they were watching Mark and me, but I hadn't really cared at the time. "But we're human. Surely there's nothing interesting about us."

He continues despite my embarrassment. "To be completely honest, there is something about the two of you that called to me—the others as well—before you even got into the Jelliad. They had some very interesting information to impart to us, which is what we want to share with you."

He tugs on my arm to get us moving again, but we don't have to go very far. At the end of the corridor is a large set of double doors, and they are cracked open. I hadn't been paying attention, consumed with my conversation with

Xane, but I'm assuming this is where the other four went.

Xane pushes one open, and we enter another room. This one is unlike the sex dungeon we left behind. I gaze around, taking in all it has to offer. Soft drapes fall from the center of the ceiling to line the walls, giving the room a bedouin tent feel. In the middle of the room is a sunken, circular area filled with cushions. Off to one side is a low table with cushioned seating around the edge, and on the opposite side is a lush grotto with a bubbling pool of water. The lighting is low, and the smell of incense lends an exotic ambiance to the room. It's intimate and inviting and quite seductive. Crimson and Savannah drag Mark down into the pit, and the three of them make themselves comfortable, though Mark still looks awkward and tense.

"Go to your man. Let us explain everything, and then you can decide how you would like to proceed," Xane whispers in my ear.

"Proceed?"

"Yes, whether you choose to go up to your room and stay there for the night."

"Or?" I ask a little breathlessly, not sure if I want to know the alternative.

"Or allow us to have our wicked way with you both."

"All of you?" I stutter, looking at the other three aliens in the room, and I feel a shiver of excitement run down my spine.

"Oh yes, honey. We don't do anything separately. It's either all or nothing." Xane saunters over to Aura, and I watch, riveted, as he grabs their chin and angles their head, slanting his lips over theirs. The two of them kiss. It's slow and seductive, and when I look at Mark to see his reaction, he's just as riveted as I am. They break apart, and Aura is breathless.

"Oh, my gorgeous warlock. You do know how to distract a person," they scold lightly, giving him a pat on the bottom. "Why don't you get us all drinks, and we can get to telling these two what's what," Aura suggests.

Xane smiles and gives them another quick kiss on the mouth before raising a hand and snapping his fingers. Another table appears in the middle of the cushions. On it are a couple of carafes and some cocktail glasses, as well as a big shisha pipe. Crimson leans in and picks up one of the hoses, putting the tip to her lips before breathing in and then exhaling. The smoke is blue, and it curls around the three in the pit before drifting into the air. Savannah claps her hands together and wiggles her body, her joy bringing a smile to my lips.

"Cocktails! What a wonderful idea, Xane." She leans forward, grabs one of the carafes, and starts pouring it into the glasses. The liquid that comes out is shimmery and pink, and once it settles into the glass, it starts to smoke ever so slightly.

"Come, Susie. Join us, and I will tell you a

magical tale." Aura and Xane step down into the cushioned pit and wave for me to join them. "We won't bite… unless you want us too." Aura throws their head back, laughing loudly before snapping their teeth at me playfully.

CHAPTER TEN

Savannah

I pour cocktails into the glasses for everyone, just to keep myself distracted from all the information and emotions that are swirling around in my head. Mark is possibly the crown prince of Celestia. This changes everything. I knew when I had my hands on him that he had a great capacity for love, but I thought he was just one of the rare humans who did. I never imagined he would be the long-lost royal child. The royal family will be beside themselves with joy when they are notified. I can imagine King Jotan will cut a path through the council to find out who was involved, because it had to have been an inside job. Maybe Xane's cousin Xavier can see if he can reach deeper into his memories than the Jelliad could. Maybe there will be something in his subconscious with a hint of who may be responsible.

My hand starts to shake with excitement, and I splash some of the liquid onto the table. I startle as a big, tan hand reaches for the carafe and takes it from me, taking over when I fail to finish the job. I look up, and Mark has a quizzical look on his face as he finishes filling the last glass.

"Are you okay, Savannah?" he asks as Xane, Aura, and Susie join us in the pit. Xane and Aura sandwich Susie between them, and I see Crimson snuggle into Mark's side. I hide my amused smile as he lifts an arm and casually pulls her into his side, not even sure if he realizes he's doing it. She smirks at me, and I poke my tongue out at her.

"Kind of... Not really. The Jelliad had some interesting information to tell us," I start.

He frowns, putting down the carafe. "It seems like you might be a bit upset about the information. Come here." He holds his other arm out, and I shuffle over the cushions, and he pulls me into his side and hugs me tight, still frowning. "Why do I have this overwhelming urge to comfort you two? And why am I not more concerned about the way Susie is snuggled into Xane and Aura? Like, there's no jealousy at all. I don't feel like I'm being influenced like I did when I was in the... Jelliad. That was an alien species, wasn't it?" He sits up straighter but doesn't release his hold on Crimson and me. She reaches around his waist and grabs hold of one of my hands, trying to reassure me the best she can. Vilaxians aren't really known for their emotional outbursts, but she does try.

"Ah, yes, where do I start?" Aura muses, playing with a lock of Susie's hair, twirling one of the curls around his finger as Xane strokes her arm with his hand. Although she looks relaxed, I can see the alertness in her eyes. "So the Jelliad imparted the knowledge of aliens to you both, but Susie, you already had some knowledge that was hidden. Right?"

"Yes, I remember everything Lila told me now."

"Okay, let's start with what we are and then we can get into the rest. Is that okay?"

Both Susie and Mark nod their assent, so Aura continues. I feel Mark's hand drift to my hair, and he starts to play with it while he listens to Aura tell him about each of us. It makes my nipples pebble with desire, but I also kind of melt into him. I love the feeling of being cherished and taken care of.

"Okay, so I know that the Jelliad downloaded all the race information into your brain, so all I have to do is tell you what each of us is and you should know everything you need to. Xane is a warlock, the same as your friend Lila's partner Xavier."

"Are you in his harem?" Mark asks quickly, obviously having all the information needed about warlocks.

I stiffen at the implication, and I hear Crimson growl.

"Did I say something wrong? Shit, I'm sorry," he apologizes quickly, and Aura holds their hand up.

"Now come on, girls, he doesn't know any better. We have to give him a little leeway to ask things."

"What did he say that was wrong?" Susie pushes Xane's hand away and sits up.

"Harems are usually a transactional arrangement with no regard to feelings for any of the parties." Xane shrugs his shoulders unapologetically.

"Yes indeed, and what Xane shares with the three of us is so much more. We are in a loving, committed relationship. Yes, he feeds from us, and we willingly and lovingly allow him to. We are not his intimate, but we are as close to that for him as we can be." Aura beams at our warlock, all the love they feel for him obvious in their eyes.

Mark nods his head slowly and brushes a hand through his hair. "Okay, I apologize if I was insulting, it's not how I meant it."

Xane waves his hand. "It's fine, I know you didn't, but the girls are a little touchy. Other races assume I can't love anyone but my intimate, but it's simply not true, and they are so rare these days that it would be horrible going through life waiting to find your intimate and not sharing love with anyone else. Aura is actually the… I guess you could say the central figure of this group. Their race is polyamorous, similar to the Skarrians, though they have no mate marks like they do. A Morpheian bites their intended mate to seal them into the relationship." Xane turns his head and points to the wicked silvery scar on his neck that matches mine and Crimson's.

A Morpheians's bite is no joke. It's the equivalent to a shark bite to humans, so you have to be serious to want one. The Morpheian mate scar fades until it's only just visible on the skin, but if the mate is approached unwillingly by another, the scar will light up bright red, advertising they are taken. It didn't do that when we were flirting with Susie and Mark because it was through our own choice.

"Morpheian? Now that's a race Lila never told me about, and I don't seem to have the information in my brain about it." Susie looks to Mark, and he frowns, shaking his head.

"No, neither do I."

"That naughty Jelliad. I guess they are a little bit of a trickster after all," Aura grumbles, pushing a loose curl back off their forehead and sighing loudly. "Morpheians are from the planet Morlash. We are a race of shapeshifters. Metamorphs can take on any shape or form we desire. In our natural form, we are a blank slate with no discerning features, and we are hermaphrodites, so every one of us has the ability to reproduce."

Aura is fairly matter of fact, but I know they don't like to talk about their natural form. The only time I remember them assuming it was to give us our bite marks. They can only do that in their natural form. I know a long time ago Aura was a captive and abused, but they do not like to talk about it.

"Although I can assume any form, we all usually have a preferred one. This is mine. I like being both a man and a woman." They are a little bit defensive in the end. They have been given a lot of grief over the years by other Morpheians for not choosing one or the other, but why should they? I pull away from Mark when I see them cross their arms defensively, waiting for their rejection, but before I can move, Susie pushes away from Xane, shuffles closer to Aura, and wraps her arms around them.

"You should be exactly who you want to be. There is nothing wrong with it." I see Aura melt into her, and I turn my head to see Mark's reaction. There's no judgment on his face, just soft eyes and a smile as he watches his girlfriend comfort our master.

"Susie's right. As long as you're happy, then that's all that matters," Mark assures them, and they are all smiles again. They make themselves comfortable, laying their head in Susie's lap and closing their eyes, and she runs her hands through their loose curls. Such a whore.

"Crimson is Vilaxian," they continue once they

are comfortable. "You would know them as vampires."

Susie's eyes widen, and I feel Mark stiffen minutely before he relaxes once more. Thank fuck for that. It could have gone badly if they had upset Crimson.

"Did you fix the cut on Susie's head?" Mark asks, and it's Crimson's turn for her eyes to widen in surprise.

"Yes I did. One of the active agents in my saliva heals." I can see her brace for reaction, but all he does is remove his arm from me and wrap both around her, hugging her tightly.

"Thank you. It was as bad as I thought it was, wasn't it?"

"Yeah, it was pretty deep and bleeding quite badly. It would have definitely required a few human stitches."

Mark squints at Susie's head. "Did you heal it completely? I thought there was still a little cut there."

Xane raises a sheepish hand. "I made it look like there was, but you can see through that glamour now. You would have been suspicious if it was gone completely. Crimson healed it completely."

"A sanguinista. You drink blood?" It's Susie's turn to ask a question. There is no fear, just pure curiosity, and I marvel at how amazing these two humans are being. I'm a little suspicious, however, that maybe the Jelliad added a bit of sedation to their healing so they wouldn't overreact to anything they hear.

"Yes, and yes, I feed from all three of my partners. They are everything I need to sustain myself. I have yet to find my blood rose, and very much doubt I ever will, because they are almost always Vilaxian."

"Okay, so that leaves Savannah." Mark reaches for his cocktail glass and takes a long drink before lounging back on the cushions, reaching for my hand. I take it, still surprised at how open and affectionate the two of them are being.

"Savannah is a Celestian. You would think of them as angels." Susie gasps and leans forward, practically smothering Aura with her robe-covered breasts, but they don't seem to care if the smile on their face has anything to say about it.

"Angel? Do you have wings?" She gasps and quickly slaps a hand over her mouth. "Sorry, is that rude? It's just some of my favorite romance books are about angels and, well, I've always wanted to know what it felt like to be wrapped in an angel's wings."

A small giggle escapes me at her enthusiasm, and I shake my head. "It's not rude. Celestians are very proud of their wings. I have mine away because they cannot be glamoured." I stand up and release the hold I had on my body. It starts to glow its normal light, and I feel my wings unfold from my back. The magic behind wings is a mystery. Technically there isn't enough space on an angel's back for them to be tucked up under the skin, and when an angel dies, their body turns to gold dust, so there is never anything to autopsy. Our skin is near impenetrable, so experimenting on us is fairly impossible too.

I shake them out to ruffle the feathers, feeling a breeze rush through them at the movement, and I sigh at the sensation. My wings are large, with over a ten-foot span, so it really is quite uncomfortable to have them tucked away. A stray purple feather drifts to the ground. It must be from the top, because it is quite dark. My feathers ombre from dark purple to white at the base so I can always tell where I lose one from by the color. A hand brushes across the base of them, and when I look down, Mark is gazing at me with awe.

"They are beautiful, just like you," he murmurs, and Susie has shoved Aura off her lap and is stepping toward me. I hold my arms up and gesture for her to come forward.

"Come here. Let's make one of your fantasies come true." My voice is husky with desire. She doesn't know that Celestians only wrap their wings around their sexual partners because it's a very intimate thing, but if this all goes where we want it to, it's not going to be a problem anyway.

She bites her lip and looks down at Mark who grins and waves her forward. "Come on, what are you waiting for? You've always talked about wanting wings."

She still looks unsure, but she steps forward until she is in my arms.

"You know if you drop your robe, the feathers will feel amazing on your naked skin," Crimson suggests cheekily, and I scowl at her, but she just shrugs. Of course she wouldn't care how much that is going to tease me. I stifle a groan as Mark reaches up and undoes the tie on her robe and shifts it back off her shoulders. It falls down and pools on her feet, and he sits back, allowing me to wrap my wings around her, cocooning us in a wall of feathers. Her naked body presses against my mostly naked one, and I shudder, enjoying how it feels. She's too busy looking around to notice, but then she reaches up and strokes through the feathers, and I can't stop the groan that leaves my mouth.

She jerks her hands away and stammers an apology. "I'm sorry, I didn't realize it would hurt."

I shake my head and meet her eyes. "It didn't," I tell her and let her see how much she turns me on. My body's glow turns purple, like my wings, and although I'm usually submissive to my partners, I can't stop myself from wrapping my arms around her and pulling her body flush against mine. "It didn't hurt at all," I assure her before lowering my mouth to hers. I press a kiss to her lips before swiping my tongue along the seam of hers, asking for entry. Slowly, she opens up, flicking her tongue out to meet mine. My feathers ripple, brushing her naked body, and she squirms in response to the light tickling sensation.

Our kiss turns heated, but I know she needs to have all the information before we go any further, so I pull away, feeling a little dazed by everything. She blinks a couple of times, before running a finger over her lips.

"My lips tickle," she says a little dreamily, and I giggle.

"Yeah, I have the ability to make things feel good with my mouth. Crimson says getting head from me is a whole otherworldly experience."

Susie's cheeks darken as she blushes and looks down at the floor. She bends down and picks up her robe. As she ties the belt, she looks up and winks at me. "Well, maybe you can show me that later."

I'm so surprised, my wings fly up and out violently, and I stumble like a juvenile angel with their wings for the first time.

"Oh my goodness. What did you say to Savannah that startled her so much?" Crimson is on her feet, ready to defend me, but Susie steps over to her and whispers in her ear. Crimson's expression changes from wary to downright sinful, and she's chuckling like a loon when Susie pulls away.

"Eat dragon shit," I tell her and flip her off in the human way before settling down next to Mark again. He and the other two remain quiet, and I don't need them asking questions, so I quickly control the conversation.

"Well, now that they know what we are, surely you should tell them the rest," I suggest to Aura, as I settle my wings comfortably behind myself and take a delicate sip of my own drink to keep my hands busy.

"Was it everything you thought it would be?" Mark asks his girlfriend lightly as she settles down and takes her own glass. I can see Aura pout at not being able to lay their head in her lap again, and I roll my eyes. Such an attention seeker.

Susie swallows her drink. "Everything and more," she says just as I take another sip, looking me straight in the eye. I choke a little bit, and Mark quickly smacks me on the back, but all he manages to do is wring another moan from me with his hand on my feathers. He quickly pulls back and looks down at his hand in confusion.

Xane starts to laugh. "Savannah has clit wings. Not all Celestians get them, but some of them are extra sensitive, and it's like they have a direct line to her clit. Our little angel is very responsive," he purrs and blows me a kiss.

Mark's cheeks turn a pretty pink as he blushes and puts his hand in his lap a little awkwardly now that he knows what touching my wings does.

"Enough of all of this. Let's finish the information session so we can get on to the fun part." Aura stands up, brushing off their fishnets and booty shorts, and straightening their bustier over their breasts.

"While you were in the Jelliad, they discovered something about the two of you. Something that both Xane and I had been feeling since you arrived. Something that shouldn't have been there if you had been human. But you're not, so that explains that."

CHAPTER ELEVEN

Susie

Aura's statement is met with silence and a heaping pile of disbelief from Mark and me. "We're not human?" my boyfriend scoffs. "Yeah, I think you made a mistake there. I think we'd both know if we were from somewhere other than Earth." He chuckles, and I can't help but join in. I'm feeling emotionally wrung out from everything, and the cocktail has a heady kick, so I'm also feeling the effects from that too. Together, it's making me somewhat giddy.

"Oh no, Susie is from Earth, but you, you sexy snack, are most definitely extraterrestrial with an emphasis on the extra." Aura's eyes sparkle, and they waggle their eyebrows mischievously. "The Jelliad scanned you, and they are infallible. You, my good doctor, are Celestian, just like Savannah."

Mark's chuckles break off, and his mouth drops open. "You're serious? You actually think I'm an alien like all of you? But I have no powers and definitely no wings. There isn't a feather on my body, and I should know, since the small amount of hair I do have is kept well manscaped." My boyfriend sounds a little hysterical by the end of his small tirade, but he is right. He does manscape to perfection, and there isn't a feather to be seen. He has very little hair too, which I appreciate immensely.

"That's the Celestian in you. We don't have a lot of body hair," Savannah comments conversationally.

Mark jumps to his feet and tries to pace around the pit, but the cushions make it too hard, so he climbs out, and the rest of us watch as he stalks around the boudoir, trying to get his thoughts in order. He pulls his hair and mutters quietly to himself, and I start to worry. I get up to go to him, but Xane stops me.

"Hang on, let Aura finish the story."

"According to the Jelliad, you are Celestian, and they can tell that you were brought to Earth. They were not able to ascertain who brought you to Earth, just that you were. The reason you have no powers or wings is because Celestian children are powerless and wingless until the age of six, and need to go through a ceremony to have both their wings and powers activated. You were kidnapped before this ceremony, so you have never had that."

Mark stops pacing and sinks to his knees in shock. Again, I try to get up, but Aura beats me to it. In the blink of an eye, they disappear from their perch in the cushions and reappear on the ground next to Mark. They wrap their arms around him, rubbing their hand up and down his back, cooing words of comfort.

"Let me go, Xane." I struggle against him, needing to help my boyfriend through this.

"Hang on, poppet. There's more."

I sag in his arms. How much more is Mark going to be able to take before he breaks?

"Mark." Savannah climbs out of the pit, her beautiful ombre purple wings rustling behind her as she moves toward Aura and Mark. "Celestians keep track of their flocks very carefully. Flocks are what we call our families. The only Celestian to ever go missing in the past thirty years is the crown prince —the child of the royal family flock. He was stolen out from under their noses mere weeks after he was born. The royal flock has been inconsolable with grief."

I can see Mark is still trying to process this information, so I jump in. "So you think Mark is this royal child? And what is the royal flock?"

"The royal flock consists of two queens and three kings. Celestians reproduce differently than humans. Celestian families are also polyamorous, so to produce a child, everyone needs to contribute, so to speak, toward the child. Although it still requires intercourse, each male will deposit their seed into the two females, and then the two females will lie together, and while they make love to each other, a magical process takes over. It takes the genetic material from all parents, combines it, and deposits it into the female who will be the birthing parent."

"Ah huh... Huh." Now it's my turn to be stunned into silence, and Xane chuckles.

"That's not even the weirdest reproduction process that the galaxy has to offer. The Jelliads reproduce asexually. They kind of just sprout a lump, which eventually breaks off and grows a new Jelliad." Xane's random information kickstarts my brain again.

"So Mark's an angel? A royal angel?"

Savannah nods emphatically. "Yes, that's what I think. Aura is going to contact the Celestian royal family and let them know about Mark."

"Hang on!" Mark shouts, and everyone looks at him. "Do I get a say?"

"Of course you do, but if it were you and your kid, wouldn't you want to know that they were alive, especially after mourning them for twenty-eight years?" Crimson says dryly, and Mark looks a little ashamed.

"Yeah, you're right, it's just a lot."

"Well, how about we let you digest that, and we can tell Susie what is going on with her?" Aura helps Mark to his feet and then escorts him back into the nest of cushions. They pour him a fresh drink and hand it over, encouraging him to have a sip. Savannah settles next to him and takes his hand, her own glowing as it sits in his.

"What is she doing?" I ask Xane, nodding at the glowing joined hands.

"Giving him some peace to help him assimilate the information without stress and shock making it harder for him."

Oh, that's good. Sometimes Mark gets stuck in his own head and is his own worst enemy when he's worrying about shit.

"So, poppet, you want to hear all about your alienness?" Xane brings my attention back to him, and I get momentarily lost in his gorgeous purple cat eyes. He and Aura are a fucking lethal combination for the senses. Then I comprehend what he said.

"Me an alien? Hardly. The closest I'll get to being an alien is my tentacle dildo, which I have in my drawer back home," I overshare and stare down at my drink. *Wow, that's potent.*

Xane's eyes light up at that, and he whistles. "Oh, you are a kinky bitch, I like it."

"Ha, hardly, that was Lila's influence. She was obsessed with kinky alien romance."

"And you never used it?" Crimson puffs on the shisha again and blows out smoke rings that curl around to look like octopus tentacles before drifting up into the air.

I shrug. "I never said that." The three of us

giggle, while the other three still give comfort to Mark.

"I'll tell you, since Aura seems to be besotted with your boyfriend," Xane states with no hint of jealousy, just amusement. It seems like nothing fazes this warlock. "What did Lila tell you about Skarrians?"

"That they were one of the first inhabitants of Earth. That they crash-landed here, and with no way to return and no access to the waters of Skarr, they lost their powers."

"Yes, that's right. The Skarrians' source of power is a ball of energy that sits within their chests and is kept powered by the waters of Skarr. Now, most lost this ball of energy one generation after the crash, but occasionally there is a throwback, even though it was thousands of years ago. Normally that wouldn't mean anything, but because you were around Lila, who had her own ball of power, I think the two of you may have had some kind of reciprocal flow that kept your balls of power alive, if inactive. Your ball of power, much like Lila's, has become usable. We hypothesize that while you were visiting Lila, you had access to the waters from Skarr, and you are in the process of changing."

Xane drops that bombshell ever so casually, and I'm speechless. I just blink and breathe, frozen in surprise, unable to say anything.

"Honey bear, I think you broke the pretty girl," Crimson says, waving a hand in front of my face.

"Do you think if I feed her some of my blood, it might help?" She crawls in front of me and holds her wrist up to her mouth. Her fangs descend, and she's about to bite into her own flesh when a hand snaps out.

"Oh no, Red, I don't think she needs a dose of your blood just yet. Let her work through things first." Xane stops Crimson, and the two of them settle down to watch and wait for me to recover.

Holy shit, I could be just like Lila. Not that she even knew what kind of power she had, she still thinks she's a dud. Maybe I will be too. What do I even do with this information?

"But without access to more water, it will become dormant again, right?" I ask, and Xane shrugs elegantly.

"Probably, but you have options. We can arrange for Skarrian water to be delivered. We have done so in the past for vacationing Skarrians. You could then keep drinking the water and see what happens, but if this is what you choose, then it would probably be best if you took a leave of absence from your job and stayed here. You never know what kind of powers will present themselves, and you will need help getting control of them. Or you could just ignore it, and it will probably become dormant again, especially now that you are no longer living with your Skarrian friend."

I look at Mark who seems to have recovered

from his own shock and is now staring at me with wild eyes. He must have heard what Xane told me.

"What are we going to do?" I ask him, and the desperation in my voice is clear. "Both of us have been given life-changing information tonight, and I don't think either of us can go back to our previous lives knowing what we know." Mark nods his head in agreement. "I think we either need to have the information pulled from our brains again, because we would always be wondering what if, or we could embrace the news and make some changes in our lives and see where this ride takes us."

"Well, actually, I'm not sure we could erase the information again," Xane muses, rubbing a hand across his chin. "Both of you have already been through a mind alteration. It's not a thing we do lightly, and we never try to erase the same information twice. Brains are delicate."

"And we still have to tell the royal flock," Savannah adds, worry evident in her expression as she looks between the two of us. "Please don't ask me to keep a secret from my sovereigns."

"What will happen? Will I have to move to their planet? Will Susie be able to come with me? What about my career?" He turns to me with desperation in his eyes. "Would you even want to do that?" I crawl around the table and push Aura and Savannah out of the way. Although I've appreciated their support for Mark, I want to be able to comfort my boyfriend and assure him that no matter what happens, we are a team, and I am going nowhere. I put my hands on his cheeks and look into his beautiful gray eyes.

"I will go wherever you want. How could I go back to my life and pretend everything is normal now? It's never going to be the same again, but I'm not sad about it. It will just take a little while for us to catch up, but as long as we're together, we can conquer anything."

"As for your career, well, I'm sure we can figure something out. If you decide to go ahead and have your powers activated, you may be able to heal with your hands and will alone. One of your mothers can," Savannah tells him, and he just blinks a couple of times.

"My mothers…" I can hear longing in his voice when he says that, and I feel a pang in my chest. I know he's always wanted a family, but both Lila and I are also former foster kids, so neither of us had any we could share with him either. I think it's probably why we gravitated to one another. I would never deny him the chance to know his family. I just hope they accept us. A tear trickles down his face, and I draw him into my arms, letting him work through his emotions. I need him to know that I will always be with him no matter what.

Aura sighs wistfully. "You two are so beautiful together. Nothing can shake your foundation."

"No, there wasn't a moment of hesitation in either of them. Their emotions are so intertwined, it's almost like they are one," Xane observes, but when I look over Mark's shoulder, he has a thoughtful frown on his face, and his eyes slide to the rest of the group as well. He shakes his head though. I wonder what he can see.

Mark stops shaking in my arms, and he pulls back, wiping the tears from his eyes. "I love you." He places a gentle kiss on my lips.

"I love you too," I tell him as he sighs, turns, and settles himself back in the cushion nest.

"You know what? I think a distraction is needed. How about you come have a look at the patient I was telling you about earlier?" Aura stands up and clambers their way out of the pit. They slip their feet back into the heels they had kicked off and pull back one of the wall drapes, revealing a door.

Mark frowns. "Have you had a doctor out to see them before? What is wrong with the person?" He jumps to his feet, automatically going into doctor mode. He holds out a hand and helps me to my own feet. I tighten the belt on my robe so I don't accidentally flash anyone before reaching out and doing the same for Mark. In his haste, he hadn't noticed how dangerously close he'd gotten to flashing everyone.

"Spoilsport," Crimson grumbles good-naturedly and takes another puff on the shisha before handing it to Savannah.

"No, not yet, but you'll understand when you see them and I explain. Also, to be honest, there aren't very many alien doctors on the planet. It is a hole you could fill." Aura sounds hopeful, like they don't want this to be the one and only time we interact, and I find it intriguing that this exotic creature—all of them, really—is genuinely interested in me and Mark, even before they found out we weren't quite human. That says a lot.

"Lead the way." Mark takes me by the hand and tows us after Aura. I look back to see if Xane and the girls are joining us, but they stay put.

"Aren't you coming?" I ask, and Xane frowns.

"No, I think it's a lost cause, but Aura has their panties in a bunch and won't let this go." For the first time since we arrived, Xane has lost his cheerfulness and is downright disgruntled. Crimson and Savannah coo at him, with Crimson tossing his top hat off to the side and pulling his hair out of its restraint before gently running her hands through it. Savannah places little kisses on his neck, sliding one of her hands over his naked chest.

"Oh, honey bear, Aura isn't going to love you any less. You know how kindhearted they are and how they don't like to see any creature mistreated," Crimson tells Xane, who isn't doing a very good job at hiding his jealousy. Now I'm doubly curious about the patient.

"Hmph, we'll see." He rolls over and drags Savannah down onto the cushions, kissing her hard.

Aura rolls their eyes and throws open the door. "This way, if you please."

CHAPTER TWELVE

Mark

Susie's hand is warm and steady in mine, and exactly what I need right now. So many of my thoughts are literally floating around in space with what-ifs and what-could-have-beens that I need the feeling to ground me. I have so many questions and no idea where to start, so maybe doing something that is familiar to me might help. I can't deny that I'm also curious, though I very much doubt my Earth knowledge will be any help with an alien species. I wonder if there is a database I can get my hands on that may contain pertinent information about different races.

My mind is still whirring when I notice we are in some kind of... laboratory, but it looks like a computer laboratory. There are a number of high-tech consoles on the wall with flashing screens and blinking lights, but it's the body on the table that gets my attention. Lying on what looks like a metal slab is a blond man with a golden tan and gold, sparkly briefs covering his genitals. Apart from that, he's naked with his eyes closed. Dropping Susie's hand, I step closer, noting he doesn't seem to be breathing, and when I put my hands on his chest to see if I can feel anything, he's cold.

"Um, Aura, I'm pretty sure this man is dead. You're going to have to call the coroner."

Aura comes around and stands on the opposite side of me and smiles. "Mark, don't forget you're dealing with aliens. A coroner is just not possible, nor is it necessary, because this isn't actually a 'man.'" They use finger quotes when they say *man*. I startle at the very human mannerism, and Aura winks. "I've picked up a few things over the years I've been here. I'm not confined to the inn, after all, and shopping in Vegas is such an interesting experience."

"So what is he if he's not a man?" I ask as I take in the perfection that lies in front of us. I mean, there's not a flaw on his perfect golden skin, and his features are faultlessly symmetrical. He is beautiful.

"Ricky here is a sex bot—a cybernetic nanobot creation from Cybertronia."

"A cyborg?" I ask, trying to shuffle through the information that is now implanted in my brain. Aura leans back against another console behind them and shakes their head.

"No. Cyborgs are capable of thoughts, feeling, and emotions just like any other sentient being. Sex bots don't have any of these, they only do what they are programmed to do. I have a couple in my storeroom downstairs. They are for the Bacaclian guards. The guards are not safe sexual partners with their pincers, and I don't have any females here for them, so I purchased a couple of bots for them to use on their downtime. Thankfully the bots are self-healing, because they do get messed up. The Bacaclians are a barbaric species who enjoy hurting their sexual partners, they get off on it, so my sex bots are programmed to be aggressive and violent during sex, but they don't feel anything. They just know how to put on a good show. Do you understand?"

I nod slowly. "I think so, they are an evolved version of a sex doll."

"Yes, exactly."

"So what, exactly, is wrong with Ricky then? I'm not sure why you've asked for my opinion."

"Ricky was sent to me by the CEO of Pleasure Bot Industries. I think you met her son, Link, with the circus." Aura raises a perfectly manicured eyebrow.

"Yes, one of Lila's partners was called Link. He's the circus doctor. Really nice guy… or I guess cyborg," Susie chimes in from behind me, stepping closer to get a better look. She runs her hand over

Ricky's chest, poking a finger into his skin. "Holy shit, he feels so real."

"Oh yes, the good doctor is delicious." Aura shivers with a seductive smile on their face. "Anyway, Ricky arrived out of the blue, and I have never known Deianira to do anything out of the generosity of her heart. She's almost as cold as a sex bot. She sent a note saying Ricky is a defective sex bot, and maybe I could make use of him here at the Pleasure Inn. Something just seems odd to me. Defective sex bots would just be destroyed, and their nanobots would be recycled into a new one. Why is the queen sending me this one?"

"Have you turned it on?" I inquire, not quite sure why they asked for my advice. "I don't know anything about cyborgs or sex bots."

"I was hoping you could use this" —they gesture to all of the technology lying around— "and scan him and see if there's a bomb or anything planted in him."

"A bomb?" Susie squeaks and steps back from the table. My muscles tense in reaction to their words.

"Why would she send you a bomb?"

"Deianira and I have a love-hate relationship. We love to hate each other. Deianira hates the fact that I have as much clout in the galaxy as she does and that we are in direct competition with each other. She thinks I should be manning the Pleasure Inn only with sex bots like many of the galaxy brothels do, but I give opportunities to alien species who may not necessarily have jobs in other places. It's not a shameful career like it is on Earth. My sex workers make big money and are respected by many. We are also quite popular because no matter how much you program a sex bot, the emotions and reactions are fake, and the clients know that. Many species are arrogant, so they value real reactions to their sexual prowess. Plus, I named this the Pleasure Inn just to piss her off." Aura chuckles wickedly. "It's an added bonus. She would quickly take over this operation if anything happened to me. Having an in on Earth would be a coup for her. I could see her convincing the Earth authorities who know about us to buy her sex bots and flooding the Earth with them."

I look around at all the equipment, and I shake my head. "I wish I could help you, I really do, but I'm not familiar with any of this, and if he is carrying a bomb, I'd worry that maybe something might set it off," I tell Aura, who frowns again.

"Yes, that could be a problem."

"Why don't you ask the Jelliads to scan him?" Susie pipes up, and I whirl around to face her.

"That's a good idea. They were able to find out all that stuff about us."

Aura slouches back against the console again, looking defeated. "Yes, but that required payment."

"What did you pay?" Susie asks, and they raise an eyebrow.

"I didn't, you did. Jelliads require sexual payment. Your sex act fueled them, and to scan Ricky, they will require the same thing. While the first scan was a kind of thank you for us having them, this one would definitely be a favor, and who knows what kind of sex act they would require us to give them."

"What do you mean? Why would it make a difference?" I question, curious to learn everything I can about everything in the galaxy. Although I'm kind of avoiding thinking about my own alien status, I'm incredibly fascinated and dying to learn all I can about everything else.

"The more deviant the act, the more power they gain from it. It's all those forbidden and naughty thoughts and feelings you get when you're doing something illicit. It's like an extra high to their feeding. So while your sex act before was a decent feed for them, it was pretty vanilla as far as galaxy sexual relationships go, and it didn't give them the extra high they enjoy."

"Well, okay, so I don't see what the problem is. You just give them what they want. I'm sure there is someone here who would suit their needs. There were lots of interesting creatures out there." Susie waves her hand in the direction of the sex dungeon.

"Hmm, yes, but what if the Jelliad wants you to be involved and asks you to do things that you might not normally? For them, it would be fun to make the newbies do things they are not comfortable with. That's the added rush they are looking for." Aura has lost all of their casual joking manner and is deadly serious. It's almost like they care about us and don't want us to be upset.

I look at Susie who shrugs. "When we decided to do this, we decided we were all in. Tonight we were going to let it all hang out, and you've done so much for us already. What kind of people would we be if we didn't help you out after everything you did for us? Mark has a chance at having a family, which is one of the things he's always wanted."

"Susie's right. We are happy to help out in any way."

"Even if it means having sex with me?" Aura asks, their eyes dropping and not meeting ours. They bite their lip nervously, and I can't believe the change in them. Gone is the sexy, self-assured master, and in their place is someone who is timid and unsure.

Susie quickly grabs my hand and drags us around the table so we can both crowd the Morpheian. She puts her finger under their chin and lifts it. "It would be our pleasure," she tells them and pulls them into a three-way hug with the two of us. Susie and I wrap our arms around the delicious Aura, and I hear a quiet sob before they stifle it and return the hug. Their soft breasts press into our bodies at the same time something starts to harden below.

Wow, I hadn't really thought about the

mechanics of all this, but it is certainly going to be an experience, and one I'm excited for. I'm secretly hoping the Jelliad requires us all to fuck. In fact, if they request an orgy from all of us, that would be something. My eyes meet Susie's over Aura's shoulder, and I can see the same lust I feel reflected in her gaze.

"Come on, let's go ask the Jelliads if they will help us." Susie presses a kiss against Aura's cheek and then does the same to me. "Hopefully they haven't filled up on everyone else."

Aura pulls back, and the hint of vulnerability we saw is gone from her face, replaced by the cocky façade once more. "Oh, I can assure you the Jelliads are insatiable. On their home planet, they feed from the atmosphere, which gives them what they need, but it's like they are always eating bread and water. What we give them is like an addiction, and they can't get enough. There are illicit Jelliad feeding dens set up all over the galaxy. Deianira is always trying to get them shut down, but I think there's enough sex in the galaxy to go around, and it's not doing any harm. The Jelliads get what they need, and the people having sex get an added kick to the act. It's just taking money out of Deianira's pocket, and that's the bottom line."

I step back and look at the metal slab Ricky is lying on. It has no wheels. "How are we going to get Ricky out there?" I ask, and Aura pushes a few buttons on the console at the head of the slab.

There's a whirring sound, and the table legs disappear before it starts hovering freely. They push another button, and when they start walking away, the table follows.

"Cool! A hover table!" The words escape before I can stop them, and Aura grins, patting me on the cheek.

"You are so freaking adorable." They lean in and place a kiss on my lips.

Their lips are soft and gentle and somewhat hesitant, so I quickly push against them, kissing them back.

They pull away and blink owlishly at me in surprise. "Oh dear, I think I might be in trouble," they mutter almost too quietly for me to hear, but I do. They whirl and stalk out the door, the table following after them.

I startle slightly when Susie grabs my hand before I look down at her, grimacing. "Sorry, I'm not sure what came over me."

"Oh, don't you dare apologize. That was h-o-t, hot. Remember, we agreed that anything goes, and to be honest, there's something about this group that attracts me. It's not that they are all gorgeous, that's just a bonus, but it kind of feels like we're supposed to be part of their group. I also can't wait to see their lips wrapped around your cock." She shivers lustfully and drags me along after the table.

I think about what she said. "Fuck, Susie, that's just it. Not once did I ever consider saying no to any

of them about anything. I wanted to please them—
no, I *needed* to. That's not like me at all."

"Right? You're the first person to tell someone
to go away when they hit on you when we are out.
I'm the same, but both of us haven't even blinked at
anything. Sure, we agreed anything goes, but
neither of us has hesitated even once. I'm almost
certain if we were at a sex club back home, neither
of us would have been as blasé about it all. Yeah,
they said the smoke lowered inhibitions, but there's
none of that down here, and I still feel no
reluctance."

"Maybe that's the Skarrian power that is now
active in your system. They are a polyamorous society," I remind her, and she claps her hands together
once before pointing at me.

"And it sounds like Celestians might be as well,
so it's our inner natures at play. But why now and
not before?" she asks thoughtfully as we stop in the
doorway to the master's boudoir. I see Aura
standing next to the pit, the table hovering next to
them as they explain to the others what is going to
happen.

"Maybe it was a side effect of the scan the
Jelliad did when it removed the mind wipes from us
and brought out our true natures."

"And how do we feel about this?" she asks carefully, reaching for my hand.

"Truth?" I ask her, and she nods, biting her lip.
"I feel good."

She heaves out a sigh of relief. "Thank God. Me too. I say we let them contact your parents and order me some water, and then let's see where this ride takes us." She sounds confident, even though I can still see the doubt in her eyes as she waits for me to respond.

I pull her into my arms and kiss her hard, assuring her that my feelings about us haven't changed. When I pull away, she's breathless and the doubt has gone. "You and me always, but maybe one or two or four more." We both turn to look at the others who are still talking about Ricky and the Jelliads.

"Oh yes," she agrees.

CHAPTER THIRTEEN

Xane

Out of the corner of my eye, I can see Mark and Susie talking about something in the doorway. I could be rude and listen in, but I figure they are entitled to their privacy. They have learned some life-altering information tonight, so the least I can do is allow them to discuss it without interference.

"So you're going to ask the Jelliads to scan Ricky? You know that's going to cost you, right?" Crimson asks Aura, who shrugs nonchalantly.

"I know."

"And if that payment requires our new friends' involvement?" Savannah presses, and we all look in their direction again. Mark has Susie in a lip lock, and I can't stop the groan that escapes my mouth.

"I want to be in that sandwich," I mutter, and Crimson bumps my hip with hers.

"Don't we all? And that is the underlying problem. The Jelliads are going to read our innermost desires and request that we give them that."

Aura doesn't look concerned. "I have already explained the situation to our guests, and they are more than willing to make any sacrifice required."

"Really?" I ask skeptically, and they nod.

"Yes, it seems like this need is not one-sided like we assumed, or at least that's the impression I got."

Savannah claps her hands joyfully and jumps to her feet, her ample breasts bouncing delightfully in her skimpy outfit. I'm momentarily distracted, we all are, until her giggle breaks us from the mesmerism.

"Well, what are we waiting for? Let's get this show on the road." She scrambles out of the pit as I slowly get to my feet, offering my hand to Crimson. Even though she needs no such help, I still like to offer it because I know she occasionally likes to feel delicate. I purposely pull her hard, and she ends up plastered against my chest. Leaning in, I take her mouth with mine, deliberately cutting my lip on her fangs. She groans and laps up the welling blood. My cock hardens, and the tentacles at the base become active at the motion. I can't wait to see how Susie and Mark react when they see me naked, or Aura— that's going to be interesting.

Neither Crimson nor Savannah has anything out of the ordinary on their bodies, but Savannah's wings are fun to play with, and Crimson's fangs have aphrodisiac venom if she wishes. I hope the humans let her bite them, she will love that if they do.

Savannah and Aura have already left the room and are heading down the corridor, but Crimson and I wait for Susie and Mark to catch up.

I just want to double-check that they are aware of the deal. You know how Aura gets, and the last thing I want them to experience is rejection. They have been through too much to let a couple of semi-humans upset them, I tell Crimson in her mind.

Good thinking. They do seem attached to these two already, and I wouldn't want what happened with that Darklarian elf to happen again. They might not recover. Crimson sounds angry when she mentions the last being the master was interested in adding to our group. We later found out they were a spy from a Darklarian warlord who was interested in invading Earth. They were just here to gather intel. Crimson made sure they never returned to report back and then informed the Vilaxian empire who destroyed the warlord's enclave, stopping any chance of invasion.

I've never seen a Vilaxian gorge themselves on a full being before, but Crimson drained them of every drop of their blood without using the aphrodisiac venom, so every swallow was like knives flowing through their circulatory system. The elf screamed the whole time, and I had to take their voice when it became too much. Crimson went into a blood coma after that for three days. We were worried, but when she woke, she said she would do it again to protect Aura.

Aura was never quite the same after that. They'd already had a horrific upbringing, and this betrayal made them question their judgment once again.

They were kidnapped as a teenager and sold into sex slavery aboard a moving starship that made it difficult for authorities to track. For four years, they were used and abused by their captives. They were a unique attraction in that they could assume any form they were ordered to, and if they didn't, they were beaten within an inch of their life. They became complacent and compliant and suffered from Stockholm syndrome. They believed they were beloved by the head trader and would do anything for them. In reality, they were just a commodity. When the warlock strike team I was a part of boarded the ship and corralled them all, Aura refused to surrender. They made themselves into a Yalani, a fierce creature from the planet Iceen, and protected their captors until I managed to invade their mind and knock them unconscious. Out cold, they reverted to their natural Morpheian state.

Even in that form, I was attracted to them. I

wanted to help them and took a leave of absence from the strike team to help nurse them back to health. Their fragile state of mind needed a gentle and skilled touch, and with my heritage, I had the power to help them. It took a long time for them to trust me, but we eventually moved from friendship into something more. Once I helped them reclaim their sexuality, I heard of the brothel opening on Earth. I thought it would be a good opportunity for them to give others in their situation a chance to thrive, and they were in agreement, so we moved here.

Crimson and Savannah were both brothel workers, and they both have their own tragic backstory. Savannah is a product of rape and was abandoned at a young age, and Crimson is so antisocial, she couldn't find a clan to connect with, so she needed an alternative option to feed. The Pleasure Inn was an answer to both of their problems.

They appealed to our need to nurture. Savannah, pretty and pliant, and Crimson, commanding and dominant, were already an established couple when we took over. Inviting them to play with Aura and me became a regular thing until Aura asked to bestow a Morpheian mating bite on all three of us, permanently joining us together. Once we became a committed quartet, they stopped seeing clients.

As Mark and Susie reach us, I cross my arms and stop them in their path. "Do the two of you know what you have agreed to? Aura does not take other lovers carelessly. This means something."

Although it's an invasion of their privacy, I listen into their thoughts for any signs of duplicity. I will do anything I can to protect our lover from more hurt. To my relief, however, I find nothing but excitement and anticipation in both their minds.

"We sure do, and I am looking forward to seeing what your asshole feels like wrapped around my cock." Mark winks at me boldly before he and Susie push past, leaving both of us speechless.

"Holy shit!" Crimson whispers and grabs my arm, squeezing it tightly.

"Wow. I wonder if they realize that not everything is normal below our clothes," I say to her a little self-consciously as my tentacles writhe in delight at Mark's words. We follow behind them and exchange a look before we both hurry to catch up. I link my arm with Mark's, and she does the same with Susie.

"Maybe a little anatomy lesson is needed before we do this, because it's a real mood killer when you strip naked and your potential sexual partner runs screaming from the room," Crimson announces matter-of-factly.

Mark stumbles, but I steady him and chuckle at his wide-eyed surprise.

"I'm sure we would be fine, but if it makes you more comfortable, then sure," Susie tells Crimson.

"Savannah and I have bodies and genitals like

you. The only extras are Savannah has wings and I have fangs, and I like to bite my sexual partners." Crimson smiles, exposing her fangs, but Susie doesn't even flinch. She just reaches out to touch one before gasping when the fang slices through her fingertip like it's butter. Before she can pull away, Crimson grabs it and sticks it into her mouth, catching the drop of blood welling on the pad. She closes her mouth and sucks hard before drawing Susie's finger out with a pop. Susie groans in tandem with Mark and myself.

"Whoa, they are sharp," she says once she recovers from her lust, looking down at her finger which has healed with Crimson's venom. "That's very cool. But why does my finger tingle?"

Crimson releases her hand and starts walking again. "That's the venom in my saliva. It has healing properties, and I can make it as pleasurable or as uncomfortable as I want."

"Well, I don't mind if you bite so long as you make it feel good," Susie tells her, and Crimson grins wickedly.

"Oh, I can make it feel really good."

"What about you? I notice Crimson didn't mention you and Aura are normal," Mark comments, and I can only hope he stays curious after I explain my added extras.

"I have tentacles," I announce. There is no point in beating around the bush. They'll either be intrigued or disgusted.

"You do?" He doesn't hide the surprise in his tone, but he doesn't sound put off either, so I forge ahead.

"At the base of my penis are a bunch of small tentacles that I can use to stimulate my partner."

"Oh yes, they are a lot of fun," Crimson calls over her shoulder. Her and Susie are slightly in front of the two of us. "Just wait until he uses them on you."

"Okay, well, that's not a big deal." Mark shrugs nonchalantly, so I see if Aura is going to be a deal breaker.

"And you can see that Aura's form is part man, part woman. They have breasts and a cock, but beneath that, there is also a vagina, and they have no testicles."

Susie and Mark are quiet as they take in this bit of information.

"If this bothers you, I'm sure they would assume a form that's more desirable to you," I add in a rush, but then I internally cringe because if they can't accept Aura how they are, then there really is no point in us attempting anything. That wouldn't be fair for Aura. They don't mind role playing for fun, and we do this often, but we also accept her in her preferred form. No one wants to feel rejected in their preferred form.

Mark's face is horrified by the time I finish suggesting that Aura could change. "God, no. We wouldn't want them to do that."

Susie stops and turns around, shaking her head. "No way. They are sexy as fuck the way they are, and both of us don't mind either sex, so really it's a win-win. Aura is a bisexual's dream."

"Susie is not wrong. Aura is perfect the way they are." We have arrived back at the dungeon. The sounds of sex are loud, echoing through the room, but Aura has enhanced hearing.

Did you hear that? I say into their mind, and I can hear their smugness echo back.

Apparently I'm perfect, they reply, buzzing with excitement. Unfortunately, they have had their chosen form rejected before by a race supposedly more enlightened than the human one.

The six of us gather around Ricky's hovering table, looking at the dungeon. The room is still filled with creatures partaking in various sexual acts. The musky smell of sweat and sex fills the room, and I can see that four of the five Jelliads are currently occupied. The one Susie and Mark had been in previously is currently being vacated by the same creatures that had climbed in after them.

The Gumblastian race's sex act is a long and tedious one that involves extensive stimulation of glands on their bodies to encourage the sexual organs to appear. Their rubber-like bodies then stick together once they join, and there's all sorts of weird grunting and groaning for another long period of time. It's kind of strange and nothing I've ever wanted to experience for myself. I know that sounds judgy considering I have tentacles, but it seems like a lot of work, and the gratification at the end appears anticlimactic.

Aura stops the next client from entering. The two-headed Snarklish snarls, both mouths showing their rows of teeth. Their partner, a scar-covered Pistadon, chatters their annoyance. The birdlike creature would have ruffled feathers if they actually had any, but they are naked and look like they have been plucked. They only have a few red and gold feathers around their cloaca to protect it.

Aura just raises an eyebrow, and I step next to them, crossing my arms, and the two of them back down. Both of them paid top dollar for me to produce a glamor charm for them to stay on Earth for an extended time. They know I can deactivate the charm faster than they can say space pants.

They hustle away and get in line for one of the others, and I hear the chuckling echo as the purple creature in front of us vibrates with amusement. *It is fun to watch you throw your weight around.* I can see by the way both Susie and Mark wince that the voice is projecting into their heads too. *What is it you wanted to ask?*

Aura waves the table over and gestures to the sex bot lying motionless on it. "I was sent this as a goodwill gift, but Deianira doesn't do anything out of the goodness of her heart."

The Jelliad's chuckle echoes once more. *No she most certainly doesn't.*

"I don't trust it, and I was wondering if you could scan it to make sure it's not a bomb or anything before I activate it."

The Jelliad is quiet for a moment before answering. *I could do that, but it would require payment. What are you willing to give me?*

Before Aura can answer, Susie steps up and puts her hands on her hips in a fierce stare down with the blob-like creature. It's almost like she's trying to protect Aura.

"We are willing to pay whatever you require."

Ha-ha-ha. The Jelliad vibrates with its laughter. *The baby Skarrian has a backbone and is protective of the master. This is just too interesting. Well then, what I require is for all six of you to fuck. I want to taste the orgasms from every single one of you.* The Jelliad's tone turns a little lecherous, and I see Susie's nose wrinkle adorably, grossed out by the sleazy creature. It is quite a coup for the Jelliad to have Aura submit to their whims. Never before would they have agreed to expose us or themself to other creatures. Our love is a personal and private thing, but their safety is our priority, and although the Jelliad has to watch, I can make it more comfortable for everyone involved by clearing the room.

I wave a hand, and the dungeon falls into silence as I freeze everyone in place before making an announcement. "Thank you all for attending this evening. Please make your way back upstairs where you may retire to your room for the night. If you have hired one of our pleasure team, they will join you and attend to your needs. The Jelliads will hopefully become a regular occurrence, so if you missed out tonight, then you will be first in line on the next occasion."

Waving my hand once more, I unfreeze the room, and the sounds of grumbles and complaints are the next thing we hear, but not too loudly because they know we won't tolerate disrespect. The Bacaclian guards move in and hover menacingly, snapping their pincers to get the crowd moving, and soon they are making their way to the elevator.

The four occupied Jelliads must turn up the orgasm juice, because the creatures inside quickly make sounds of finding their releases and then are evicted onto the floor in front of the blob they had been in. It takes these creatures a little longer to get moving, but soon enough, the dungeon is cleared out with only the five Jelliads, the six of us, and Ricky remaining.

Because there are so many of you, we will join to provide you with a larger area. The other four Jelliads move toward the one in front of us, their weird, undulating movements unexpectedly quick. They stop just short of it then flow together, making us all step back as it grows in size. There's some groaning sounds, and the blob momentarily turns opaque before gradually clearing to a translucent purple again. *Also, scanning an inanimate object is harder than an organic one, so my people will assist. Are you ready?*

The six of us exchange a glance, and everyone nods their assent. "Let's do this," Aura announces before they bend down, pick up Ricky in a bridal hold, then climb into the Jelliad.

CHAPTER FOURTEEN

Aura

It's not easy to maneuver Ricky and myself through the gel, but Xane quickly follows me in and helps. We lay Ricky out and to one side as the three girls and Mark join us. The Jelliad potency soon starts to penetrate my skin, and I begin to tingle, my sexual attraction building, but there's a kind of awkward mood surrounding us. It's not something born of ease like it would be with just Xane and the girls. No, this is a new path, and while usually confident in my sexual prowess, I'm still a little wary about starting something.

We stand around looking at each other, the giant combined Jelliad big enough for all of us to do just that.

Suddenly, Susie starts to laugh. She doubles over, holding her stomach and wiping at her eyes.

"God, this is awkward," she says around the laughter before getting a hold of herself and pulling off her robe. We made the mistake of not stripping before entering. She holds it out in front of her, pushing her shoulders back confidently, and shakes it at Xane. "Can you take care of this and all of that?" She waves her hand around, gesturing to all of our clothes, and a grin creeps across Xane's face before he winks at her.

"I like how you think." He waves his hand, the movement made a little slower than normal due to a slight resistance from the gel, and suddenly, we're all naked. Strangely enough, my hands go down and I cup my cock, not wanting them to see how different I am down there compared to normal men.

Susie leans in and whispers something to Mark too quietly for me to hear, even with my advanced hearing. They have a quick conversation before kissing one another. We watch the two former humans as they break apart, and then Mark moves in Savannah and Crimson's direction, while Susie heads toward me and Xane.

I feel my eyebrows jump as Mark wraps an arm around each girl and drags them into him. Slowly, he lowers his head and takes Savannah's lips with his own. Tentatively, he runs his tongue across the seam of her lips, and I watch as my little angel melts against him, her wings ruffling seductively behind her. Crimson reaches up and strokes along one tip, reaching her other hand down to wrap it around Mark's rapidly hardening length. The two of them moan into each other's mouths with her touch.

My own cock hardens, and I can no longer cover it with my hands, but Susie is in front of me now, and she catches my hands, pulling them away from my body. "Don't hide yourself, you're beautiful," she whispers reverently as she takes in my body.

She's shorter than I am, even without my heels on, and her mouth is right at breast height. With her eyes still on mine, she leans in and licks one nipple, and I feel my legs wobble. She cocks her head to the side, like she's asking if she can continue, and I quickly nod as Xane steps behind me, the two of them boxing me in.

She lavishes attention on both my nipples, and I can feel my breathing and heart rate increase as Xane slips his hand between Susie and me and wraps it around my cock. He strokes the length slowly, and I turn my head so we can kiss. The mood has definitely changed now, and all it took was the two former humans being bold. Thank fuck for them.

Susie pulls back from my nipples and grabs my chin. She tugs my mouth from Xane's and down toward hers. Her lips are soft and full against mine, and she tastes divine. I can feel Xane watching us, and his grip tightens minutely on my cock as we exchange soft, exploring kisses. She pulls away, and her eyes sparkle with lust and joy as a grin spreads across her lips.

"You taste amazing." She runs her tongue across her lips, chasing the taste of me. "Oranges and spice," she murmurs, and Xane laughs.

"That's Aura's thing. They taste like your favorite flavor. To me they taste like whiskey and smoke. To Crimson, Aura tastes like her favorite blood type. All her bodily fluids taste like that." Susie's eyebrows jump on her face at Xane's words, but she's soon scrambling to her knees in front of me.

"I guess I should see if he's telling the truth, shouldn't I?" A shout from the other three has us all turning our heads. Mark is sandwiched between the two girls much like I am, with Savannah on her knees already bobbing her head up and down on his cock, but it's Crimson's fangs in his neck that caused the noise. We watch as Mark's eyes roll backward with every sip she takes. He grabs hold of Savannah's head and thrusts hard, the talented angel taking everything he releases into her mouth, unable to stop with Crimson's venom flowing through his system.

My attention is quickly brought back to my own ménage à trois as Susie runs a tongue along the length of my cock. I shudder at the sensation, but she sits back on her heels and frowns. I feel myself shrink inward and away from her, waiting for the rejection now that she's down there face-to-face with all that is me. I brace myself for the words I know are coming and try to cover myself, but she slaps my hands away.

"Xane, hold Aura's hands please," she commands, and he chuckles quietly but does as she says. "Can you also move them so they are reclining? I don't have the best angle."

"Of course I can, poppet," he purrs and pulls on my shoulders, moving me backward through the gel. My legs automatically go up until I'm in a horizontal position. I'm sort of half sitting and half lying down, but I have a perfect view of Susie sliding my thighs apart before she slips between them. She shuffles her body forward, placing tiny, nipping kisses along one thigh until she gets up close and personal with my genitals. I brace myself once more for rejection, but she just smiles wickedly, wraps her hand around my cock, and leans forward, running her tongue through my slit.

Throwing my head back, I groan loudly and feel my mouth morph into my original form, my need to mate bite Susie coming out of nowhere as my mate venom drips onto my tongue. The sharp, possessive taste makes me struggle to get at her. Xane's eyes widen, and he leans in, kissing me fiercely and allowing me to bite him. Tasting his blood brings me back to my senses, and my mouth morphs back to my preferred one.

"No mate bite without permission," he scolds

me before kissing me again. His tongue slides sensuously against mine, then he nips and sucks my lips much like Susie is doing to the lower ones. As quickly as he started, he pulls away, leaving me breathless.

"If you slide your tongue just inside the top of their slit, that's where you will find their clitoris. Unlike a human's or the girls', theirs is internal," Xane instructs Susie. She releases my cock and uses both hands to spread my thighs wider. Xane moves around to join her and takes over pleasuring my shaft, his talented mouth engulfing me down to the root as Susie uses her tongue, poking it as deeply as she can and sliding to the very top of my slit, finding one of my pleasure centers. At the same time, I feel Xane slide a finger in just under her tongue, covering it with my natural lubrication before he drops it lower and plunges it into my asshole.

"Fuck!" I shout, and I can't help the automatic thrust of my hips. My cock surges down Xane's throat, but he just hums, creating more vibrations, and Susie continues to lash my clitoris with her tongue, sliding two of her own fingers in where Xane's had been. With all of my pleasure centers being stimulated, there's nothing I can do but lie back and enjoy the ride. I thrash my head back and forth as I moan, chanting their names. My orgasm is building to its peak, my entire body tingles with anticipation, and my toes curl as it gets closer.

Having Xane's hot mouth around my cock and Susie's fingers and tongue inside my slit are almost too much for me to take.

"Don't come yet," Xane orders, pulling off my cock then replacing his mouth with his hand. The onslaught of pleasure is almost too much for me to bear, and I grit my teeth, holding back my release like he demanded. "How do they taste, Susie?" Xane asks her, running his spare hand through her hair before gripping her curls and pulling her away. She looks dazed, her mouth glistening with the evidence of my pleasure. My cum is slightly intoxicating, giving the receiver a drunk feeling.

"Amazing. I want more." She tries to return to what she was doing, but Xane holds her hair tightly, and she blinks owlishly at him.

"Let's swap, and you can get a better taste when they come," he tells her, taking control. I knew it wouldn't be long until he took over. He doesn't like to be submissive. Normally I don't either, but I'm not complaining.

They swap positions, and Susie slides her hand up and down my shaft, her tongue playing with the underside of the tip of my cock. That really sensitive spot has me thrusting my pelvis up into her hand, needing more friction, but Xane slaps one of my thighs, the sting causing me to yelp and stay still. He slides three fingers into my slit, stuffing me full, before returning two to my asshole. The groan that leaves my mouth is guttural and desperate.

"Please," I beg.

"Do you hear that, Susie? They plead so prettily. How about we give them what they want?" Xane coos, and she engulfs my cock with her mouth. She can't get as far down as Xane—it's long and thick and takes some working up to—but she wraps her hand around the base to assist. Then, in tandem, they work me to a peak again. This time I don't hold back, and I fly right off the edge into a double orgasm. My cunt squirts, covering Xane in my cum, at the same time my cock erupts into Susie's mouth, and she enthusiastically swallows it all down, moaning her own enjoyment at the taste. It seems to go on forever, the orgasms battering my body with pleasure, and all I can do is ride it out, my head thrown back and eyes closed against the onslaught. I'm breathing heavily by the time the sensations finally wane, and when I look between my legs, Xane and Susie are kissing sloppily, sharing the taste of my cum with each other.

"Oh my god, you were right, it does taste different for you," Susie exclaims as she pulls back from him. She uses her tongue to lick around his mouth, cleaning him up from where I squirted all over his face.

Before she can get it all, Crimson moves into sight, pushes Xane out of the way, and kisses Susie who startles for a moment but quickly responds. Crimson must be chasing my taste inside Susie's mouth as she licks and sucks her lips.

"Go on, Mark, kiss Xane," Savannah says, coming around to my head and running her hand through my sweaty curls. "See how good Aura tastes." Mark slides in behind Xane, turning him so they face one another, and then the rest of us watch as Mark slides one of his hands into Xane's ponytail and pulls out the band. Xane's long indigo locks fall around his face before Mark gathers it in both hands, moving his head much like Xane had done to Susie, and holds him in place while he cleans up his face much like a cat cleaning their kitten. Long, confident strokes of his tongue clean up all of my release from Xane's face.

"Fuck, they do taste good," Mark mutters and moves closer. Xane uses both hands to grab both of their cocks, stroking them in tandem. "Didn't I tell you I wanted to feel your asshole wrapped around my cock?" he says to the surprised warlock. "How about I fuck you while you fuck Aura and they fuck Susie?" he suggests, and Susie claps her hands.

"Oh yes, and Savannah can sit on Aura's face, and I can take good care of Crimson. A six way! Surely that has to be enough power to scan the sex bot." The former humans don't wait for our responses and take charge. Susie crawls up and over, straddling my body. She kisses and nips my nipples again before leaning forward and kissing Savannah above me. The two of them giggle as their hands explore each other's breasts, and I feel a mouth on my cock, but I can't see who it is since Susie is blocking my view. The scrape of fangs soon solves that problem, and I know it is Crimson. She nicks my cock with her fang, and I feel her venom seep into my body, my cock throbbing even harder now, but I lose sight of everything as Susie helps Savannah straddle my head, and she lowers herself down. My hands come up to grip her thighs, and I morph my tongue so that it splits into two. One half is long and thick, and I slide it up into her pussy so she can ride it like a cock, while the other half is thin and forked, and I flick it over her clit. Savannah groans and grinds herself down on me, and I smile. I love giving my partners all the pleasure they can handle and then a little more.

Crimson

My tongue and fangs torture Aura's cock as Savannah slides into position. I can tell by her guttural groan that Aura has morphed their tongue into our favorite shape, and Savannah can now ride it like a second cock. I pull away from the one I'm giving attention to and slide my hands onto Susie's waist. I help her turn around so that she's facing me, and then I hold the base of Aura's cock for her to slide down onto reverse cowgirl style.

Aura's cock is thick and long, so it takes Susie a couple of goes, bouncing up and down until she's completely impaled by it. I lend a helping hand by supporting her breasts as she bounces, twisting her nipples. Her mouth drops open, and her eyes roll slightly. Her pleasure is gorgeous to see, but she's finally fully seated.

Xane comes around, his cock in hand, and stands in front of Susie, holding it out for her to lick, so I lean in and get in on the action too. The two of us coat his cock with our spit between kissing each other and his length. A pair of hands come around and cup my breasts, and Mark expertly pinches my nipples until I'm vibrating with need as well. My fangs throb in time with my clit, and I can't wait to sink them into someone.

Xane pushes our heads away and sinks down onto his knees, sliding his dick deep into Aura's slit. Their muffled groan causes Savannah to groan as well and bounce up and down a little faster. Once he slides in, he pumps back and forth as he and Susie alternate when she goes up on Aura's cock and Xane slides deep.

Mark removes his hands from my breasts and appears in front of me. He pushes me down onto my knees and feeds his cock into my mouth. "Be a good girl and lube me up?" he asks, winking at me. I'm not one to normally be submissive, but I do enjoy a cock in my mouth, and my fangs make it all the more fun. I lick and suck a couple of times, but then I slide my fangs into the vein on the underside of his cock. He shouts and thrusts forward as I allow my venom to run into his bloodstream. I take a couple of sips of the warm, delicious blood, but then I spread it around so the blood coats his cock —instant lubrication that's better than any spit. I help him to his knees and push Xane's back, making him bend slightly. His face ends up in Susie's breasts, and he pays them lavish attention as I help Mark breach his asshole. The blood helps him slide right in, and he's quickly seated deeply. Xane and Mark groan in tandem, and I shudder as I step back and watch the five of them join as one. As much as I want to have Susie's mouth between my legs, I also want to sink my fangs into her neck and get another taste of her nearly Skarrian blood. Before I can make a decision, Xane speaks up, his tone rough as Mark slides in and out of his ass, which also pushes him in and out of Aura.

"Aura, honey, Crimson doesn't have anything to ride. Can you help her out? I think she wants to bury her fangs into Susie's neck."

Aura's body vibrates slightly, and just above where Susie is sitting, they produces another long, fat cock.

"Holy shit," Susie mutters, looking back over her shoulder. "That is fucking amazing." She slides off the one she's on, turns around, and slides back onto it. Leaning forward, she takes the spare one into her mouth, sucking and licking before pulling back. "There. It's ready for you," she announces and holds her hand out, helping me straddle our lover and assisting me to ease down over the spare cock.

Her finger circles my clit, and she bounces up and down on her own cock, her breathing getting heavy. "I'm so close," she calls out. "It's all too much seeing everyone fucking."

As if her words are a signal, everyone picks up the pace. There is no more speaking, just a symphony of grunts and groans as we all chase our pleasure. My pussy flutters, tightening around Aura's spare cock as Susie pinches my nipples hard. I do like a bit of pain with my pleasure. I lean forward, pushing her corkscrew curls off to the side, and run my tongue along her neck. Without warning, I strike, sinking my fangs deep. Her skin makes a slight popping sound as my fangs penetrate it.

I inject the orgasmic venom before retracting my fangs and sucking hard on the wound, drawing her sweet, fulfilling blood into my mouth. It proves to be too much, and she screams, setting off a chain reaction, all six of us finding our pleasure at once. My cunt pulses with each swallow as I bounce up and down on Aura's dick, drawing out the pleasure as long as possible while I watch my partners around me writhe in ecstasy.

CHAPTER FIFTEEN

Susie

The Jelliad starts to vibrate as the six of us come down from our sexual high, becoming coherent and cognizant once more. Groaning and undulating, the Jelliad writhes wildly, and I gasp, grabbing hold of Crimson's arms in fright. She just strokes a reassuring hand over my back. Aura's cocks are still lodged deeply inside our pussies, and they are still hard despite them finding their own release. "It's okay, the Jelliad is scanning Ricky now that we've juiced it up."

"In more ways than one," Savannah says breathlessly from over Crimson's shoulder. She pulls herself off Aura's face, and I watch in amazement as the cock tongue she'd been riding and the one that had been pleasuring her clit morph back into a single muscle and shrink down to normal size.

Mark and Xane chuckle at Savannah's suggestive remark, their bodies still intertwined. Mark's cock is still buried in Xane's ass, and he gives an occasional thrust, causing Xane to grunt. My own needy cunt flutters around the cock still inside me. There are so many things I want to do with all of these people that I feel a pang of regret that our time together may be limited. If Mark and I go on to discover our own alien origins, they will remain on Earth running the brothel, but I really don't want to be separated from them despite this all being so sudden.

Xane must feel my drooping emotions, because he wraps his arms around me from behind and nuzzles into my neck where Crimson bit me. It's still throbbing slightly, but that pain stops when he presses a kiss to it. "What upset you?"

Before I can answer, the Jelliad stills.

"Huh, that was quick." Aura sits up, and Crimson slides off her spare cock, which again melts back into Aura's body. They wave a hand, encouraging all of us to move, so I slide off their dick. I feel the evidence of their orgasm drip down my thighs as I move out of the way. Crimson and Savannah quickly come over and lick up each thigh, catching all that Aura left. I want to grab hold of their heads and shove them into my pussy, but something tells me we don't have time, so I fist my hands by my sides and watch Mark dislodge himself from Xane, who does the same to Aura. Finally, we are all individuals again.

Aura crawls over to Ricky, who is reclined out of the way from our extracurricular activities. The evidence of Xane's own pleasure dripping out of their slit below their cock, and I have to stop myself from going over there and running my tongue through the mess. What the fuck is wrong with me? My need for these people is beyond anything I've ever felt. Mark comes over and wraps his arms around me.

"Are you okay?" he whispers in my ear, and I grit my teeth and nod.

"Yes, but a part of me is desperate to fuck and claim every one of these people over and over again until I make them mine. I don't know what is going on with me," I whisper as we watch Aura run their hand through the sex bot's platinum blond hair and sigh.

"So tell me was I right about him being a booby trap. It would be a shame to see such an exquisite specimen destroyed. He would have been very popular as part of my stable."

I'm not sure if Aura actually means the words coming out of their mouth. They seem a lot more invested in this sex bot than just as a sex worker. They seem soft and kind of wistful when they look at them, as well as slightly possessive, which is how I feel about everyone.

He is not a booby trap in that he is a bomb or dangerous,

the Jelliad announces somewhat cryptically, and Aura frowns.

"What do you mean?"

This is not a sex bot, but an actual cyborg. He has had a spell put on him to make him mimic a sex bot with no feelings or emotions, but it's fake. He should wake up soon once he recovers from our scan.

I can tell by Aura's wide-eyed, taken aback reaction that they had no clue, and they look kind of speechless, so while they compose themselves, I ask a question.

"So you're telling me Ricky is a fully sentient being like all of us?"

Crimson wraps her arms around Savannah, mindful of her wings, leans her head on her shoulder, and strokes her hand through her messy blonde hair. They must have the same burning need for affection and physical touch I have.

Yes.

"What is that bitch up to?" Aura mutters, exchanging a glance with Xane whom I feel shrug.

"I have no idea, and who has the kind of power to spell a cyborg like that? I'm almost a hundred percent certain that it's not a warlock."

You are correct. The spell was not warlock in origin. There is another magical race at the very edge of the cosmos, the Seiomann. They have subjugating types of powers and would be capable of this, but they have been kept in check by the Vilaxians. Their movement is restricted to their home planet, and they are not allowed to travel space due to them taking the Aaz'ax's side in their war against the Unas. There is a Vilaxian warship that ensures this, and the warlocks created a barrier around the planet that is impenetrable if you have Seiomann DNA. Though that does not stop people from visiting the planet, the Jelliad shares, and I see this is new information for everyone but Crimson who nods her head.

"Yes, I did six months on that warship during my public service. Any Seiomann that manages to get past the barriers is shot down by the ship. It doesn't happen all that often, but occasionally one will try."

"So does that mean Deianira and Ricky both traveled to that planet?" Mark asks as he nuzzles my neck.

Yes, baby Celestian, you are correct.

Before any of us can ask any more questions, Ricky moans, and his head moves before he gasps and sits upright. "I'm free?" He looks around the Jelliad, his gaze falling on Aura. His eyes widen in surprise at the sight of the naked Morpheian. Without hesitating, he throws himself at Aura. Xane tenses and lifts a hand to freeze him, but he's not quick enough, and Aura is enveloped in the arms of the now sobbing cyborg.

"Thank you, oh thank you so very much. I thought no one was ever going to figure out what that evil woman had done all because she doesn't like to be told no."

Aura wraps their arms around him and looks at

us over their shoulder. Aura melts into a puddle of goo as they coo at the little lost lamb in their arms. Xane chuckles quietly when he sees the look on their face.

"That's it, I'm pretty sure our group is going to grow from six to seven."

Our group? "You include me and Mark in your group now?" I ask, turning my head so I can look at him, and his eyes widen minutely before he sighs.

"Yes. I had to stop Aura from biting you during our orgy. I had to remind them that they need your consent before making life-changing decisions for you," he confesses quietly, and I feel my own eyes widen in shock, but before I can respond, I hear Ricky talking again, so I pay attention. I want to know how he came to be here too.

"I was hired by Deianira to be her personal assistant. It's not the job I applied for. I wanted to work on programming, that's my specialty, but I figured it was at least a foot in the door and I could hopefully transfer. She continuously made passes at me, telling me that I would be fired unless I had sex with her. I told her to fuck off and that I was going to take the information to the board and her husband. She didn't scare me, she was just a bully. She pressed a button on her desk, and before I could leave her office, I was arrested by her internal security and shoved aboard a starship. The last thing I remember is this floating creature in a cowl, with three red eyes, looking at me. She was there.

She told me if I thought I was too good for her then I needed to be taken down a peg or two, and what better way to do it than be used by every manner of creature, and if it helped bring you and the Pleasure Inn on Earth down at the same time, then that was a bonus." He pulls out of Aura's arms and looks around, not appearing too concerned about being trapped in the Jelliad. He looks back at Aura. "I know you're Aura Gasm, owner of the Pleasure Inn, so I guess part of her plan succeeded, but my body doesn't feel any different, so I'm assuming I haven't been 'used' yet?"

"No, I was suspicious of Deianira's motivation, so I asked the Jelliad to scan you. I thought you may be a booby trap."

"I was under the impression that Jelliads were not allowed on Earth," Ricky replies, sitting back on his heels, and Aura shrugs.

"They are not, but I have my ways."

"Fuck!" Ricky runs his hands through his blond hair, making it stick out in all directions. "Deianira planned to report to Earth Alien Authorities that you had an illegal, unregistered cyborg in your business. That's what the trap was meant to be. I would have reactivated when the raid leader gave the right code word. How long have I been here?" He sounds panicked now, and everyone else has finally come down from their sex high and are looking worried too.

"You arrived this morning," Aura tells him, and

everyone springs into action. The seven of us exit the Jelliad, and Xane waves a hand, cleaning and clothing everyone, including Ricky. He puts us all in comfortable sweats, and Mark throws an arm around my shoulder as the Jelliads groan and grunt and separate once more.

"She was reporting you tonight because she knew you had an event happening." Ricky looks around the sex dungeon, not appearing particularly perturbed, but I remember Lila saying that cyborgs were very sexually inventive, so I guess this is nothing for him. He stops when he gets to Mark and me, and his mouth rounds in surprise. "You have humans here? How? I didn't think it was allowed!"

Mark's arm tightens around my shoulders, and Xane and Aura exchange a glance. "I'm thinking this is all way more than a coincidence," Xane states, not answering Ricky's question. "You said two of your tires were flat, right?" he asks us, and Mark nods. "The likelihood of that is slim. What if this is all a setup and your tires were shot out deliberately? If the Earth authorities were to find humans and an unregistered alien, that would be enough for Aura to be shut down and deported."

Aura is scowling. Their sweats sit deliciously low on their hips, and the tank top they are wearing hugs their curves and rises just slightly, showing the gorgeous V leading to their equally gorgeous cock. They are distracting as all hell, and it's really hard for me to concentrate on everything that is happening. I think I still have sex brain and orgasm fog. No one else seems to have the same problem though. Crimson has started herding the Jelliads in the direction of the elevator.

"We need to get you out of here. We can't have anyone finding you here or asking questions about how we got you onto the planet," she tells them, and they follow obediently, not wanting to get caught by the humans.

We will be in touch, the lead one announces as they depart.

"How did you get them here?" Mark asks, voicing what I had just been thinking.

"They worked out a way to hide their ship by tucking into the Galaxy Circus mothership and cloaking. When they teleported to the ground, the Earth Authorities just assumed it was one from the circus. It was easy and how we have smuggled things onto the planet in the past. We just don't abuse it and can only do it when they are here," Xane explains as the rest of us head in the direction of Aura's personal elevator.

We pile in, and Mark pulls the gate closed behind us, then we start to ascend. Before anyone can say anything else, a siren starts blaring, and red lights flash. "Unauthorized person on the property," a voice announces. The elevator comes to a stop before it's supposed to.

"Damn it!" Aura shouts. "Xane?"

"Move closer and put your hands on me," Xane commands, and we all move forward, doing what he said. "Hold on tight." He starts to dissolve into mist, which seeps out and around, covering us all. There's a lurching motion, and I groan as my stomach somersaults. When the mist clears, we are in the front lobby of the inn.

I stagger, and Xane helps me to a nearby chaise while Savannah does the same for Mark. The two of us lean on one another as the others talk out a game plan over the sound of the sirens.

"All the other clients here tonight are registered and capable of glamour, right?" Aura asks Xane and Savannah.

"Yes, I made sure of it myself when they booked," the blonde Celestian replies, twisting her hands in agitation.

"Good, they all need to assume their glamours in case whoever this is wants to raid the rooms. I'm pretty sure I'm the target, but I want them to be prepared. There are some human authorities who would gladly shut this operation down and kick us all off the planet."

Xane and Savannah hurry off to check that everyone is doing as they should. "Fuck, the Baca-clian guards need to be glamoured too," Aura calls after them, and Xane waves a reassuring hand.

"I've got this," he shouts back, and Aura sags in relief. Ricky jumps to support them and gets a gratefully, if distracted, kiss on the cheek in thanks.

Mark and I watch as Ricky lifts a hand to where Aura just kissed with a look of complete awe and devotion on his face. The awe clears, and a look of determination replaces it. He gets down on one knee and bows his head.

"I owe you everything. I am yours to command," he vows to Aura, and Mark snorts.

"He needs to be careful what he wishes for."

Ricky must hear him, because he slowly turns his head and looks him dead in the eye. "No I don't. I would be grateful for any scrap of attention Aura gave me," he announces fiercely, and Mark flinches.

"Oh dear, you upset the pretty cyborg. You're going to have to do some groveling now," I tease him, and he grumbles.

"I didn't mean it badly. I like it when Aura commands me."

Aura blows a distracted kiss at Mark and helps Ricky to his feet. "We can reassess this at a later stage. For now, I need to figure out what I'm going to tell them about you three." His wave encompasses us all, but we don't get a chance to brainstorm as the door blasts open, flying back off its hinges and hitting the reception desk.

A tall, fierce-looking man steps through the doorway with his hands held out, pulses of power circling them. Behind him, a swarm of men clad in black fatigues with weapons I have never seen before hurry in, surrounding us.

"Aura Gasm, you are charged with harboring

humans and an unregistered alien. This goes against the agreement to allow you to operate on Earth. On behalf of the Earth Alien Authorities, you and your staff are under arrest. Any aliens also on the premise tonight will be deported and denied re-entry to Earth." A tall human male, who's wearing a black suit and Ray-Ban sunglasses despite the fact that it's night, steps around the troops holding weapons on us. He looks around the room as if he's looking for someone before looking at Aura. "Where is your master?"

Mark and I exchange a confused look. Aura flutters their eyelashes seductively and pushes out their breasts, and I realize what is happening. The man obviously hasn't met Aura before and is looking for a male, and at this moment, in their tight tank top with their boobs almost overflowing, Aura looks very much like a woman. Luckily, the man is so distracted by that he doesn't look any farther down. They discreetly adjusts their sweats, pulling them up and hiding their washboard abs.

"Why don't you just wait here, and I will go see where they are?" Aura whispers girlishly, and the man nods.

"The house is surrounded, so don't even think of making a run for it. I have instructed my troops to shoot any of you creatures on sight."

Aura nods and hurries away. The alien with the power still flowing through his hands moves his feet, looking bored. The human turns to him and holds up what looks like a remote. He pushes a button, and a collar around the alien's neck lights up red. He grunts and groans, and the power in his hands flicks out as he drops to his knees. One of the black-clad soldiers hurries behind him and uses the butt of his gun to knock him unconscious. The collar around his neck fades, disappearing from sight.

"Get him back to his cell," the man with the remote orders as the glamour that was covering the alien fades, leaving behind a being unlike any we've come across yet. He retains his humanoid shape, but he is covered in spikes, long and short. If I had to compare him to anything from Earth, I would say he looks kind of like a lionfish that I'd seen in an aquarium once. The long spikes have sheer membrane draped between them. There isn't any hair on his head, just a crest of spikes, but it's his color that is stunning. He looks like an opal, all greens, reds, blues, yellows, and pinks.

"Holy shit," I hear Ricky whisper. He stares at the alien before stepping slowly backward, sliding toward Mark and me. When he gets close enough, I reach out and grab him by the hand, tugging him down between us, protecting him. The man with the remote is still distracted by the stunning alien being dragged away.

"What's wrong?" I mutter under my breath.

"Apart from the obvious?" Mark adds unnecessarily. He gets grumpy when things are out of his control.

"That is an Aaz'axian. They have another form as well and if you see that one, you need to start running. They are supposed to be wiped out. How did one come to be on Earth and controlled by the Earth Authorities? That is dangerous," Ricky says just loud enough for the two of us to hear. "Something else is going on. Nothing good can come from this."

CHAPTER SIXTEEN

Mark

Susie, Ricky, and I stay quiet and motionless as the lead human looks around the room. He holds out a hand, gesturing toward the rest of the mansion. "Flush them out. If they fight, don't hold back," he orders his men, and most of them disappear down the corridor, their feet pounding on the wooden floors as they infiltrate the Pleasure Inn. Not much later, screams and shouts echo down to us as they start to enter bedrooms occupied by Aura's clients.

Ricky shudders and huddles closer into the two of us, whimpering. Whatever this poor cyborg has been through has obviously scarred him, and I can tell by the stubborn set to Susie's jaw that she is not going to let anything happen to him. I stand up as the man in front returns his attention to us. I step slightly in front of Susie and Ricky, blocking them from view.

"What the hell is going on here? My fiancée and I had a flat and found a room for the night. There's nothing illegal going on, just a party, a costume party. I think you may have bad intel. Aliens, ha-ha-ha," I huff in fake amusement, but the man just ignores me.

A commotion down the hall has us all looking in that direction. Crimson has found a tailored pencil skirt and jacket and is looking professional with her red curls pulled back into a bun at the base of her neck. She's carrying an iPad and escorting a man I haven't seen before.

He's tall and deadly handsome, with sharp cheekbones and an aristocratic nose. His hair is chestnut brown with a hint of curl and a short, stylish cut. The pinstripe black suit, lovingly clinging to his slender frame, fits like it's custom made and expensive. He has a haughty look on his face and stares down the military leader with disdain.

"What seems to be the problem?" he asks in a cultured accent that is not quite placeable.

The military leader looks him up and down, raising a skeptical eyebrow. "You are Master Gasm?" he asks, and I do a double-take as I realize Aura has assumed a different form to appease the authorities.

"I most certainly am, and who the fuck are you?

Do you have an ID or a warrant to explain why you are barging into my place of business?" they demand, putting a deceptively casual hand into their pocket.

"I'm Agent Smith, and I don't need a warrant, as we don't recognize you as Earth inhabitants, and as such, do not need to follow the laws." The man removes his Ray-Bans and tucks them into his pocket, revealing watery, pale blue eyes.

"You are under arrest for harboring an unregistered cyborg and two humans, which are against the regulations that we stipulated when we allowed you to operate this place of ill repute." He wrinkles his nose like he's smelled something bad. "You will be deported and banned from returning to Earth. The circus is here, so you will be transported to a holding cell, before being handed over to the Adams brothers for deportation ASAP."

Aura starts to argue, but the man holds up a hand. "If you fight this, I will have my men kill every alien on the premises, starting with the illegal cyborg and the two humans who now know things they shouldn't." He points in our direction, and I narrow my eyes.

"How do you know we are human and that he is a cyborg?"

A smug grin spreads across the agent's face. "I have my sources," he tells us, his eyes drifting back down the corridor. We all turn to look at what he's staring at, and Aura and Crimson gasp.

A pretty, dark-haired girl dressed in a satin robe and heels struts down the hall and over to the agent.

"Buttercup!" Aura exclaims, and I recognize one of their staff members from earlier who had been assisting in the dungeons. "You would betray me like that? After everything I've done for you?"

The girl rolls her eyes as she leans in and places a kiss on Agent Smith's cheek before turning and looking at Aura with disdain.

"You bet your ass I would. You run this thing like a halfway home for wayward aliens, allowing the whores to pick and choose how often they work and the kinds of clients they fuck. It's pathetic," she spits out aggressively. "With you out of the way, I will make sure this business grows rapidly and makes more money than James and I will know what to do with."

Before Aura can respond, more sounds echo down the hallway, and out pour all of Aura's clients and staff wearing human glamours and surrounded by the human military men. I see Aura slump when Savannah and Xane are pushed to the front and shoved to their knees in front of us.

"These two will be the first I kill if you don't cooperate." Agent Smith holds up the same remote he was using to control the other alien before and presses a button. Xane screams and shakes, falling to the floor and twitching.

"God, stop! Fine, just fine. We will cooperate. But just you wait. That is the warlock king and queen's nephew. You have started an international incident that you may not be able to talk your way out of," Aura warns, and the agent just smirks.

"That's what I'm counting on." He turns to his men. "Load them into the transport vans and let's get moving. Don't forget the cyborg, but leave the two humans. I'll make sure they are taken care of," he says ominously.

I get shoved out of the way by a masked man, and he grabs Ricky, shoving cuffs onto his hands. He then shoves a gun into his back and gets them moving. I don't try to interfere because I don't want anyone to get trigger happy. There's a lot of fire power being pointed at us, and that would not go well.

"They are not humans," Aura announces rather quickly as they try to herd them away from us. "Both have alien DNA, the male being the crown prince of Celestia. Again, another international incident waiting to happen. Better to deport them both than risk the wrath of the angels coming down on you." Aura is looking back over their shoulder, their eyes filled with an apology as they disappear from sight.

It's the first time that the agent looks a little concerned. He turns to Buttercup, lifting an eyebrow, and she shrugs.

"Kill them or don't, who cares," she says carelessly. She got what she wants now. She examines the aliens as they get brought out, pointing out the staff she wants to keep and clipping controlling collars around their necks before shoving them off to the side. The escorts all have looks of horror on their faces. She stops and points to the next four. "Those are the Bacaclian guards. You may want to talk to them, their loyalty can often be bought."

"I will speak to them at the detention center. For now, everyone goes, including the two not humans." He comes to a decision regarding Susie and me, and I feel her shaking as she stands up and tucks into my back. We are quickly swarmed by two guards and cuffs are placed on both our wrists.

We are herded along with the remaining clients and placed into the back of transport vans. Susie's cry of relief at the sight of the other five is heart wrenching. The seven of us have been put in the same van somehow, and we crowd close to one another, taking comfort in each other's touch. I still feel the adrenaline causing my heart to race unnaturally fast, so feeling them is comforting.

"What's going to happen?" she asks, her teeth chattering with fright.

"We will be taken to the detention center and handed over to the Adams brothers as prisoners for deportation," Xane says groggily. There's a bruise forming over one eye where he seems to have taken a hit. "Between them and my cousin, we will be fine, but something is definitely not right."

"Xane is right." Aura sounds pissed. They are still in the male form they assumed, and it's taking me a little while to adjust to it. I blink a couple of times, and they chuckle. "I know, it takes some getting used to, but this is one of my favorites too. Do you like it?" they ask, striking a very Aura style pose, and my mind seems to accept it all at once.

I nod my head. "Yes, very much." They chuck me under the chin with their restrained hands. "Such a good boy. I'll make sure you're rewarded once we get out of this mess."

"What do they think is going to happen? I just don't get it. Did you notice Buttercup was only keeping the weakest of our workers? They are going to be abused and mistreated." Savannah is teary-eyed, worrying about the underdog.

I see Crimson reach for her, but with our restrained hands, she is unable to comfort her. Instead, Savannah just rests her head on her shoulder and sobs.

"I overhead Deianira talking with the Seiomann that bound me. Something about Earth and a deal and an orb of power. I wonder now, after seeing the Aaz'axian, if there is more to this than just petty jealousy."

The other four, who had not been around to see the alien who blasted down the door change forms, gasp. "An Aaz'axian? They are extinct," Xane argues, but Ricky shakes his head.

"Nope, the three of us saw him. He's being controlled by the agent too, or he seemed to be."

"That seals it. We need to tell the Adams

brothers everything we saw and overheard. Something is fishy, and the intergalactic alliance needs to be advised. If they did have an Aaz'axian, who's to say he's the only one they have? And if they are controlling them, that could spell disaster for all of us." Aura sounds defeated for the first time since the alarm started ringing.

The door to the transport vehicle slams closed, blocking out our view of the mansion. Two more doors slam, and the truck starts up, telling me we're about to begin moving, and my stomach sinks. There's no one left to save us, and I feel myself slump. Xane sees me, and a crooked grin spreads across his lips. I can see a drop of blood well up from a split that must have come from being hit too.

"Don't panic, Doc. We may be down, but we are far from out. They fail to realize that they are taking us to allies. We have done nothing wrong, and we will not be punished for it, but I'm thinking being on this planet may not be the best place for us for now." He turns and looks at the back door like he can see the mansion disappearing in the distance. "But we will be back, even if it's to rescue the rest of our family. Buttercup had no idea how we got the Jelliads down here, and combining my power with Xavier's, we can probably teleport them without needing any mechanical assistance if need be."

"Lila will help us," Susie says with blind confidence, and I don't doubt that she is right. We will sit tight and play possum for now, but trouble is coming. and I think Susie and I need to embrace our new heritage and powers if we want to be able to help our new friends.

I lean back against the wall, Susie's and Ricky's body heat on either side of me, and wait until it's our turn. I vow that Agent Smith hasn't seen the last of me.

GALAXY

CIRCUS

GLOSSARY

PLANET ICEEN

Lightning Cats

They are a shifter race that has two forms—a bipedal human form and their cat form. Their bipedal form is humanoid in shape, but they are covered in a soft downy fur except for the front of their torso and genital area. They have sharp teeth, big ears, and long tails in this form. Their animal form is similar to a saber-toothed tiger from Earth. They can shoot lightning from their tails, and it can be used for defense and attack.

They are a matriarchal society and live in family groups called streaks. They have alpha, beta, and omega distinctions, but there is always a female alpha who acts as head of the family.

Alphas have a rut and omegas have a heat. Only alpha and omegas can breed with one another, and betas can only breed with their own designation. There are male and female omegas. Both have breeding capabilities, but male omegas are rare. Most are killed once their designation is discovered to prevent competition with females for coveted positions within the streak.

The planet Iceen is a frozen tundra of caves and outcroppings, and the streaks usually have two dwellings—a cave for their animal form, and a dome-like, insulated glass building which they live in with their streaks.

Maxsim (Alpha Lightning Cat)

The leader of the streak of lightning cats that performs in the circus, despite it being a matriarchal society. Maxsim is a dark aqua blue that ombres out to snowy white in the legs, with black, tribal style markings across shoulders, chest, and arms. He has high cheekbones, cat ears, feline eyes, a tail, and fangs, which are bigger when in animal form, as well as a broad chest and well-defined arms. Fur covers his body when in humanoid form, except for a patch across his chest and down to his groin.

Maxsim keeps the rest of the streak safe from an aggressive Natalia.

Natalia (Beta Lightning Cat)

Only female in the group that performs in the circus. She is heir to her matriarchal streak, but is a beta designation. Natalia has pale blue fur all over, with long black hair, high cheekbones, cat ears, feline eyes, a tail, and fangs. She has small breasts, a slender, toned body, and a lean backside and legs. She has naked patch across her breasts and down to groin.

She wants to form a streak with Maxsim, Trace, Fuse, and Sim, but they are alphas and cannot breed with her. She took her omega sister's place, who was supposed to be the one performing with the circus.

Echo (Omega Lightning Cat)

He is a pure white lightning cat, with a smaller frame than Maxsim's, and built much more delicately. His designation is omega, and he has survived because he comes from a rare streak with a male omega. The streak, with help from the warlocks, protected him while growing up. They hid it, and he presents himself to the world as beta. He wants to form a streak with Maxsim, but not Natalia. She discovered he is an omega and keeps trying to kill him.

Other cats in the group
    Trace (Alpha Lightning Cat)
    Fuse (Alpha Lightning Cat)
    Sim (Alpha Lightning Cat)

Yalani

An abominable snowman type creature with shaggy white and gray fur. They are good at blending into their surroundings. It is a hunter-gatherer species that lives in caves on Iceen. Eight to nine feet tall, they are an aggressive species that will attack if they feel threatened. They live solitary lives unless mated and raising a family.

PLANET SKARR

This planet is the birthplace of the human race. The original humans were exploring Skarrians who crashed on Earth, and because they no longer had access to the magical waters, lost all their supernatural abilities.

Skarrians are mostly polyamorous and have attraction marks that show up on both parties' bodies. If attraction wanes on either side, the marks disappear. Skarrians find themselves bonded to others after five rounds of sex, which requires them to orgasm simultaneously. Skarr is basically a sister planet to Earth in that it is made up of ten different land masses surrounded by pink oceans, but it has different species of plants and animals.

When reproducing, all bonded members of the family must participate to produce a child.

Lila Jenson (Liliana Adams)

Orphaned at a young age, she moved from foster family to foster family, never really fitting in anywhere, though nothing terrible happened to her. One family put her into gymnastic lessons and self-defense courses to keep her out of trouble. She has no real goal in life, but has always thought there must be something more than working in a bar and having the occasional one-night stand.

She is average height, with a curvy figure, long chestnut hair with turquoise streaks, golden skin, and green eyes.

Lila discovered she has grandparents who are still alive, and they invited her to learn their family business.

Currently, she has shown no signs of having Skarrian powers despite an impressive first showing.

John Adams, William Adams, and Eric Adams

Triplet brothers who appear to be in their late forties, they possess chestnut hair, tall, slender builds, and emerald green eyes.

They have been searching for Liliana, also known as Lila, for years, and are thrilled to have finally found her. They are also the CEOs of the Galaxy Circus and guardians of the power orb.

William has a buzz cut and is gruff.

Eric has long hair, which he wears in a man bun, and is the joker and tease in the family.

John has short, tousled hair and is the kind and

loving brother, but he is subject to spirals of depression.

Alina and Marcus Adams (Dec.)

Lila's parents moved to Earth in order to raise her in relative safety, but they were killed in a car accident. Alina had blonde hair and green eyes, and Marcus had brown eyes and the same chestnut hair as the grandpas and Lila.

Magenta

She is a performer in the circus. When on Earth, she uses the circus silks, but on other planets, she uses her levitation powers. Magenta has bright pink hair and pale skin. She is mid height with a slim build and light blue, almost gray, eyes. She has been a lifeline for Lila when it comes to all things alien.

Broderick Potter (Bubby)

Captain of the mothership and Marcus Adams' best friend. He has red hair and a red beard with crystal blue eyes. He's rugged and well-built and thrilled to meet Lila.

Phillip and Fiona

They are Lila's twin cousins, but not on the Adams' side of the family.

Fiona has long, curly red hair, brown eyes, and freckles with a tall, slim build.

Phillip's red hair is cropped short, and he has brown eyes and freckles with a tall, slim build.

They oversee the dinosaur act. The dinosaurs were hand raised in the zoo on Skarr.

Captain Lester

Captain Lester is an alternate captain for the mothership and circus pod. He has an abrasive personality and a voice like he smokes two packs of cigarettes a day.

PLANET EARTH

Susie (A Night Most Wicked)

She is Lila's best friend, with dark, mahogany skin, melted chocolate colored eyes, and black corkscrew curls. She's a nurse and previously lived with Lila.

Mark (A night Most Wicked)

Mark is Susie's boyfriend. He has black hair and gray eyes, and works as an emergency room doctor. Mark is also bi.

PLANET FLUXX

Fluxx is a sister planet to Skarr, and its waters have magical properties too, but it gives its inhabitants the ability to shift into another creature. Fluxxians are animal shifters with three forms—humanoid while retaining coloration and some features of their animal, half form, and beast form. Fluxxians can use glamour to blend in and must do this when on Earth and in public. Fluxxians have fated mates, and their animal will dictate how they reproduce.

Caspian (Kraken Shifter, Lila's First Mate)

Caspian performs in the first act in the circus, shifting into half form and juggling multiple items with his tentacles.

He has mottled blue and purple skin, piercing stormy blue eyes, nipple rings, and vivid purple hair shaved on either side with a long section on top the drapes over one eye. His tentacles are purple and blue when in half form. Caspian's beast form is large. Male krakens implant their parents with their eggs via an ovipositor, and the womb then fertilizes the eggs, basically doing the opposite of a human. Fertilized eggs can lie dormant inside the female for a long time until she is ready to give birth. Drinking a large amount of the male kraken's cum tells the eggs that you are ready for babies. Four weeks later, they are born in kraken form. Two weeks after that, they are able to shift into their human form for the first time. Krakens can have anywhere between one and six babies at a time. Non-kraken mates will have their biology changed when given the mating bite. This allows them to carry a kraken's eggs for their partner.

Dylan (Dragon Shifter)

Dylan is in the first act of the show, which is a fire breathing act where he actually breathes fire.

He has ebony skin, wings, a metallic black shimmer to his scales, yellow and green reptilian eyes, and fangs. He also has sharp cheekbones, and his nose flattens slightly in half form.

Dylan is the man whore of the circus. He befriends Lila early on, only to betray her later and get kicked out of the circus for his act of aggression.

Silac (Naga Shifter)

Silac is one of the shifters who replaced Dylan in the first act. A Naga shifter, he has tousled emerald green hair in his humanoid form, with long, lean muscles and nipple rings. His eyes are orange and black. When he is in half form, he has a snake body from the waist down, with emerald green scales covered in horizontal orange stripes and black diamonds. Naga males have a hemipenis that hooks in to hold their partner close during copulation, and their mates give birth to live young.

Tirrian (Dragon Shifter)

Tirrian is the dragon shifter who replaced Dylan in the first act. Where Dylan was pitch black, he is more like an oil slick black. He has a shimmer to his skin that flickers from green and gold to pink and blue. He appears holographic depending on what angle you look at him from. In half form, his wings are the same color and his scales are holographic pink. He is tall, broad, and muscular. His hair is black with pink streaks in it, and his eyes are black with lines of pink in them. He's an asshole.

Dragons can only have young with female dragons or their mates. Once again, a mating bite will change a non-dragon shifter mate to allow them to lay eggs. Eggs are incubated by the couple for two months before being born. They must be kept at a certain temperature to ensure a live birth. Homosexual dragons can hire surrogates to help them with reproduction if they wish, and it is common practice for young dragons to offer this service as a way to start their own hoard before they wish to begin their own family. There is a website that can help facilitate this.

PLANET CYBERTRONIA

A technologically advanced planet inhabited by life forms that are half organic, half nanobot technology, allowing them to change their features at will. Reproduction occurs through intercourse, but parents program their respective organic matter with the traits and features they wish their babies to have. Once the baby is born, their source code is imprinted on a microchip, which is then deposited into a secret storage facility for safe keeping.

Pleasure Bot Industries is one of the main sources of employment for Cybertronia. They produce lifelike robots for sexual pleasure and are one of the galaxy's most popular purchases. Pleasure Bots are not like cyborgs, in that they are incapable of thoughts, feelings, or responses that have not been programmed into them.

Link (Cyborg)

Link is the ship doctor for the Galaxy Circus and is one of Lila's boyfriends. His skin tone is peach with a shimmer. He has silver hair and eyes. He is built like a swimmer, with long, lean lines, a tapered waist, and broad shoulders, and he is able to change his body parts at will. Cyborgs can't lie.

Josa Spears (Cyborg Nurse)

Josa is the nurse to Link's doctor, but he was hired by Link's mom to spy on him and the circus. He was promised Link's hand in marriage and a share of the Pleasure Bot Industries fortune if he complied. He has the same shimmery skin tone as Link, with metallic green hair and eyes. He has a slender, feminine frame and a dirty attitude.

Deianira (Cyborg A Night Most Wicked)

CEO to Pleasure Bot Industries and Link's mother. She doesn't like to be told no.

Ricky (Cyborg A Night Most Wicked)

Sent to Aura as a gift from Deianira. Blonde hair, tanned skin and gorgeous body.

PLANET VILAX

Vilax is home to a race of blood drinkers, the sanguinistas. Much like Earth's legend of vampires, this race is strong, fast, and has heightened senses. They can fly, and are very hard to kill. Their bodies will regenerate as long as their body parts are close to one another. To kill them, you need to burn both of their hearts. They are a warrior race and one of the fiercest in the galaxy. Military service is mandatory for all Vilaxians.

Vilax only gets five hours of sunlight a day, so while they are not allergic to the sun, they do prefer the dark. Sanguinistas drink blood because their bodies cannot process their own red blood cells. They have a fated mate called a blood rose, but not everyone finds them. They live in family clans, and blood sharing can be a sexual thing, but with children, it isn't.

Saxon (Sanguinista)

Saxon is part of the aerial troupe in the circus. He has magenta-colored eyes and thick, short black hair that's long enough to run your fingers through. His body is muscular and broad, and he has pale skin and fangs.

Hale (Sanguinista)

He is in the same troupe as Saxon and is Saxon's best friend. He has blond hair, teal eyes, and fangs.

Radella (Sanguinista)

Estrella (Sanguinista)

Velorina (Sanguinista)

Xenos (Sanguinista)

Saxon's brother.

Dante (Sanguinista)

Kavita (Sanguinista)

Crimson (Sanguinista) A Night Most Wicked

Long red curly hair, tall, toned and lean. Crimson is antisocial and could never fit in with a sanguinista clan so once she finished her compulsory public service for Vilax, she got a job working at the Pleasure Inn so she would have a variety of options for feeding. Clients like being bitten during sexual relations. She was in relationship with Savannah prior to Xane and Aura taking over the brothel. Aura bestowed a mating bite on her, permanently joining her in their group and she stopped seeing clients.

PLANET WESTALIN

This is the warlocks' home planet. Warlock powers include, but are not limited to, mind manipulation and control, teleporting, and manifestation. Powerful warlocks have harems to feed from because they are psychic feeders who feed from strong emotions. Weaker warlocks and other creatures make up these harems. Weaker warlocks benefit from it, as they are able to feed off the stronger warlock at the same time and get a temporary boost in power. Members of the harem receive a wage and a comfortable position within the warlock's household. Powerful warlocks are able to absorb powers and life force, but it is frowned upon and is only used as a punishment. Warlocks have soulmates they call intimates. When a warlock finds their intimate, they no longer need a harem to feed from.

Xavier Colest (Crown Prince)

Xavier is one of the most powerful beings in the galaxy, only second to his parents. He is mostly with the circus because he gets bored easily. He helps with glamour to confuse the humans. He has purple/blue eyes and long indigo hair. His body is lean and muscular, and he has piercings in his ears, nose, and eyebrow. His ears are pointed, and he has lavender-colored skin with silver markings.

Xylene Colest

Queen of the Westalins and Xavier's mother. She was best friends with Alina and Marcus Adams, Lila's parents.

Cronus Colest

King of the Westalins and Xavier's father. He was best friends with Alina and Marcus Adams.

Xane Colest (A night Most Wicked)

Nephew of the King and Queen and former Strike team commander. Mate to Aura Gasm, master of the Pleasure Inn and powerful warlock. He has long indigo hair, shaved at the sides exposing more silver tribal like tattoos on his skull, and is tied back and there's a top hat covering it. Silver rings line both ears, as well as in his eyebrow and his bottom lip. Sharp cheekbones with eyes that look to be purple and pouty lips. Rescued Aura when they were enslaved on an illegal brothel ship.

Elyan (Warlock, Head Harem Girl in Xavier's Harem)

Nambra (Warlock, Harem Member)

She has red hair and a voluptuous figure.

Lexus (Warlock, Harem Member)

She has short dark hair and a petite frame.

Ara (Warlock, Harem Member)

Ara has pale pink hair, eyes, and skin.

Jastia (Warlock, Harem Member)

Jastia possesses buttercup yellow hair, eyes, and skin.

Sinath (Rasque, Harem Member)

The Rasque is a humanoid race that looks like an Earth grasshopper. They have segmented arms and legs with plated body structure. Their penis is covered by plated sections, which retract when manipulated. Once the penis extends, claspers lock the copulating couple together.

Mithus (Milobar, Harem Member)

He has a stingray-shaped head and body, with arms, legs, and a barbed tail. Mithus has two penises, which both have barbs that activate during intercourse, locking them within their partner.

Zanorn (Morpheian, Harem Member)

A race of metamorphs, they are able to take any shape they desire. In natural form, they are like a blank slate with limited features and gray skin.

Topirey (Dionall, Harem Member)

Dionalls are plant creatures with two forms— one is an upright humanoid sentient form, and the other is a stationary plant form which is similar to the Earth's Venus flytrap, only a lot larger and it feeds on flesh. They have leafy foliage on their head and sharp teeth, and are able to grow their body parts at will.

PLANET AQUILIA

Aquilia is seventy-five percent water, and the Aquilians are an aquatic species with three forms—humanoid, mer, and beast form. In beast form, they resemble an Earth dolphin, but are scaled and have sharp teeth. They come in a variety of pastel colors. In half form and on two legs, they retain the pastel colors and cannot glamour. They require a glamour spell if they want to tour Earth. Family groups are called pods. Aquilians rarely leave their home planet, and if they do, they will return once they form a pod so that their young are born in their home waters.

Nikos (Aquilian Prince)

Nikos is one of the performers in the dolphin show in the circus. He is a member of the Aquilian royal family, but not in line to inherit. He is arrogant and horny. He has pastel green skin, and his scales are pastel green and gold. His hair and eyes are metallic gold.

Nixie (Aquilian princess)

Nixie is Nikos's sister and also a performer in the circus. She's friendly and fun and is interested in exploring the galaxy. She does not want to get trapped by being mated on Aquilia. Nixie is also open to trying relationships with other species. Her colors are pastel blue and gold, with metallic gold hair and eyes.

Galaxy Circus Pod Members

Joaquin

Nolani

Marin

Dorado

PLANET RILU

Rilu is a desert-like planet with small green oases dotted across its land surfaces. There are no above ground oceans or seas, but there are large underground ones which provide fresh water for the inhabitants of the planet. At each of the oases, which usually center around a small lake, are wells which provide fresh drinking water for travelers. Some of the larger lakes have permanent villages established for trade. The people of Rilu are nomadic tribes. They raise larnuks and are miners. Under the surface of Rilu are extensive gem mines, and the people of Rilu mine the gems for trade and to feed their larnuks.

Larnuks

These are creatures much like Earth's Pegasus, possessing both wings and a horn. They come in the same colors as the gems that are mined on their planet—emerald, ruby, sapphire, gold, and amethyst. They eat gems and spout fire, and they have sharp, vicious teeth. They are bred and raised by a larnuk mistress or master who will bond with their herd. The larnuk will bite them, and a lock of their hair will turn the same color as the larnuk's. The more streaks a master or mistress has, the more larnuks they control.

Rilax

Rilax are berries that grow in the mines alongside the gems. The berries are used to make rilaxious, a pink alcoholic beverage popular across the galaxy. It is slightly bubbly with a thick, creamy consistency.

Zala (Larnuk Mistress)

Zala is the larnuk mistress for the circus and is in charge of that portion of the show. She has exotic, Middle Eastern looks with darker skin and wavy, pitch-black hair with streaks of color in it from her horses. Her eyes are a pale blue, almost white, rimmed in kohl, and framed with long black lashes. She is tall and slim, and her body is covered in silvery scars from bonding with her horses. Five appear in the show, but she has more.

PLANET MORLASH

Home of Morpheian race. They are shape shifter who can merge into any form, metamorphs. They are hermaphrodites and all members of the race have breeding capabilities. They usual assume a preferred form which is either male or female, Aura prefers to be both.

Morpheians are polyamorous and bestow a mating bite in their natural form to seal their mate to them. It is quite a painful process ensuring that the mate is genuine.

Aura Gasm Proprietor Pleasure Inn (A Night Most Wicked)

Aura was kidnapped by alien sex traffickers as a teenager and forced into an illegal brothel where she was regularly abused to keep her in line. Developed Stockholm syndrome and tried to defend her captors when the ship was raided by a warlock strike force led by Xane.

Xane, besotted by Aura nursed them back to health and have been together ever since.

PLANET CELESTIA

Celestian are what humans would call angels. All Celestians have wings and powers. Powers tend to be emotive in nature, healing is one of the powers, as is being able to manipulate emotions. Celestians glow with heightened emotions, the color their glowing tells what emotion they are feeling. Lavender is horny.

Celestians are also polyamorous and reproduction involves a magical process that combines everyone's DNA ensuring the child is a part of all mates before depositing the embryo into the chosen carrier.

Savannah (A Night Most Wicked)

Tall and voluptuous with a a long mane of blonde curls, and sliver eyes. Savannah is a product of rape and forced breeding which should be impossible with the way Celestians breed. She was cast out by her mother as a baby, never fitting in anywhere, teased and ridiculed. She made her home the Pleasure Inn as a way to make herself feel good. Crimson taught her she didn't need to have sex with someone to be loved.

PLANET RECCEDEA

A lush, foliage-covered, tropical planet with frozen poles on either end. It is the birthplace of the dinosaurs found in the circus. Many species of dinosaurs that once roamed the Earth continue to survive and thrive on this planet.

Ziggy

Ziggy is a red and black tyrannosaurus rex. He was trained from a baby, and acts just like a giant, overgrown golden retriever.

Vigolash

Vigolash is a yellow and orange velociraptor, who was also trained from a baby, but is unruly and kind of crazy.

OTHER ALIEN RACES

Unas

A race of highly intelligent, peaceful, powerful beings who created the power orb that the Galaxy Circus protects. The now extinct race had powers that were fueled through sexual energy. They didn't have mates or partners, it was just a free-for-all orgy.

Their war with the Aaz'ax dwindled their numbers until there were only a handful left. Their energy was absorbed into the orb when they turned it over to the Adams brothers. They used the Adams' ancestors' blood to link it to them, and if it leaves their line, anyone remaining will be absorbed too.

The power orb was supposed to be a clean, free source of energy capable of powering planets across the galaxy. It can be used as a weapon of mass destruction, but cannot be destroyed because the galaxy would implode.

Aaz'ax

The leadership of this race was cruel and vicious and wanted to use the orb to conquer other lands. They possessed it momentarily and laid waste to a number of planets, but the Unas were able to take it back. By then, the Aaz'ax weren't doing well. A mysterious illness had taken most of their women, and women of other races wanted nothing to do with the men. Their species has been on the brink of extinction and were finally able to dispose of their tyrannical leadership. Remaining survivors scattered to planets far and wide. The Aaz'ax are distant ancestors of the Vilaxians. Although they do not require blood, they can consume it, but it acts much like alcohol and drugs to a human. They have the ability to glamor, and they have two natural forms, their warrior form which is humanoid, but their shoulders and backs are covered in ridges and their body looks like they are covered in thorns. With their green skin and blood-red hair, they resemble a rose. And their everyday form which is again humanoid but he is covered in spikes, long and short. Comparable to an Earth's lion fish. The long spikes have sheer membrane draped between them. They don't have hair just a crest of spikes, but it's their color that is stunning. They look like an opal, all greens, reds, blues, yellows, and pinks.

Originally people thought they were two separate races because of how different they look.

Darklarkian (Planet Elos)

Elf like race identifiable by their pointy ears and black skin, and green snake like eyes.

Snarkle (Planet Cereabosto)

Humanoid bodies with two heads. Each head has a mouthful of sharp teeth

Pistadon (Planet Laxo)

Bird like creature similar to a pterodactyl. Sharp beaks and beady eyes, they have no feathers, look like a freshly plucked chicken. The only feathers on their body surround their cloaca. Red and yellow spike like feathers circle this opening protecting it from unauthorized penetration.

Seiomann (Planet So)

Magic race with subjugating powers. They can make it so a being can not access their powers. They also have the ability to freeze a person in stasis. They appear floating draped in a dark cloak with only discernible feature are three red eyes.

Telazions (Planet Telaz)

They sold the tech for the iPhone to Steve Jobs.

Nengh

They perform as clowns in the circus. They have detachable limbs and are able to adjust their body's size and mass. They are humanoid in shape, but they are orange with feathery tufts instead of hair. They use a glamour provided by Xavier to appear human when on Earth.

Jelliads

A race of purple gelatinous amorphic creatures. They are sentient and communicate via telepathy. They feed from the atmosphere of their home planet but they can also feed on orgasmic energy. They can change their shape and the breed asexually.

Bacalacian

From the planet Bacalac they are humanoid form in that they walk upright and have two legs but they have a red armor plated outer shell, bright red when on high alert, orange at rest. They have two pincers in place of arms, that are razor sharp and dangerous. Their torso is triangular with two eyes on stalks sticking out of the top and a mouth opening with a single pair of teeth on top and bottom which grind food between them.

DICTIONARY

Phoeall (fo-all): Warlock for…

Vigolash: Obedient one in Aaz'axian

Sandar worm: native to the planet Westalin, they are large creatures that turn soil over in their paddocks between crops. They eat all organic matter left from past crops, leaving it free for farmers to plant the next crop.

Silax worm: Native to Rilu, it lives in the mines and is a pest. Their secretion kills the rilax berry plant. They are trapped, and their secretions are used to make achom.

Achom: A drink that is like a blend of coffee and chocolate with a chili vodka kick.

GIN: Galaxy Information Network.

Karta monster: A large, kaiju style creature the size of an elephant.

Cirillion: Little bundles of fluff with big eyes.

Lastovian hog: A long pig like creature with six legs, five eyes and a piercing squeal.

Saturn's Rings: A restaurant on the mothership.

Edalaxion Space Station: A space station with dodgy bars and meeting spaces for the dregs of the galaxy.

Celesian Brothel: A popular brothel if you want to have sex with living beings as opposed to sex bots.

Jaxa bird: A bird native to Westalin, it looks like a cross between a peacock and a phoenix. Its tail is a fanned bloom of fire.

Kala mouse: A marsupial found on Westalin.

Coolmy shell: This is a crustacean found in Aquilian waters.

I know, I know that was a softish cliffhanger. But the rest of the story will cross over with Whisperer the next Galaxy Novel, Which you can pre order here Whisperer

Thank you for reading!
I hope you enjoyed the book. It would be super awesome if you could leave a review wherever you bought it, because I love to hear what you thought of the story.

Want to keep up to date with new books coming soon? Sign up to my newsletter here
Newsletter

Another way to do that is to join me Facebook group. I drop teasers and giveaways in there all the time. Here's the link
Lexie's Ladygarden

Visit my webpage and check out reading orders and what else I've written.
www.lexiewinston.com

ACKNOWLEDGMENTS

Thank you…..

Jess for your invaluable editing. For putting up with me sending it to you in two halves and then all the dramas in between, I don't know what I'd do without you.

Emma as always listening to all of my shit

My alpha and beta teams for being super awesome as usual.

And of course my friend Grace who attempts to keep my needy ass sane.

Thank you to everyone who reviews and recommends it and thank you to all of you who take the chance and preorder the next one as soon as you've finished the last. You guys are the reason I can keep writing this story.
Until next time. Happy Reading
Xoxo

Lexie

Spies Like Me

For so long now I've been a solo operative, not having to worry about anyone but my target and myself. I even have a code name that is whispered throughout the underworld.

The Phantom.

And people know to be scared if they get on my radar.

But the director of the secret agency I work for is also my dad, and I'm still his little girl despite how many kills I have under my belt. He's decided that I need to have a team to back me up.

I strongly disagree.

But we made a deal. If he wins, I have to join a

team of his choosing and work a sex trafficking case with them, leaving the Phantom to retire. But if I win, he never brings it up again and I get to stay a ghost.

I'm going to hand this team their ass, because the Phantom is not a team player

Get it now